The Journey Prize Anthology

Winners of the $10,000 Journey Prize

1989
Holley Rubinsky (of Toronto, Ont. and Kaslo, B.C.)
for "Rapid Transits"

1990
Cynthia Flood (of Vancouver, B.C.)
for "My Father Took a Cake to France"

1991
Yann Martel (of Montreal, Que.)
for "The Facts Behind the Helsinki Roccamatios"

1992
Rozena Maart (of Ottawa, Ont.)
for "No Rosa, No District Six"

1993
Gayla Reid (of Vancouver, B.C.)
for "Sister Doyle's Men"

1994
Melissa Hardy (of London, Ont.)
for "Long Man the River"

The Journey Prize Anthology

Short Fiction from the Best of
Canada's New Writers

Selected with M.G. Vassanji

M&S

Canadian Cataloguing in Publication Data

The National Library of Canada has catalogued this publication as follows:

Main entry under title:
The Journey Prize anthology:
the best short fiction from Canada's literary journals
1–
Annual.
Subtitle varies.
ISSN 1197-0693
ISBN 0-7710-4428-3 (v.7)
1. Short stories, Canadian (English).
2. Canadian fiction (English) – 20th century.
PS8329.J68   C813'.0108054   C93-039053-9
PR9197.32.J68

Typesetting by M&S
Printed and bound in Canada on acid-free paper.

The publishers acknowledge the support of the Canada Council and the Ontario Arts Council for their publishing program.

"Boy" © Elise Levine; "The Falling Woman" © Shaena Lambert; "Going Native" © Antanas Sileika; "Hand Games" © Elizabeth Hay; "Maps of the Known World" © Mary Borsky; "Of Marranos and Gilded Angels" © Kathryn Woodward; "Opera" © Michelle Alfano; "The Rat-Catcher's Kiss" © Roger Burford Mason; "Song of Ascent" © Gabriella Goliger. These stories are reprinted by permission of the authors.

McClelland & Stewart Inc.
The Canadian Publishers
481 University Avenue
Toronto, Ontario
M5G 2E9

1 2 3 4 5   99 98 97 96 95

About the Journey Prize Anthology

The $10,000 Journey Prize is awarded annually to a new and developing writer of distinction. This award, now in its seventh year, is made possible by James A. Michener's generous donation of his Canadian royalty earnings from his novel *Journey*, published by McClelland & Stewart Inc. in 1988. The winner of this year's Journey Prize, to be selected from among the nine stories in this book, will be announced in October 1995 in Toronto as part of the International Festival of Authors.

The Journey Prize Anthology comprises a selection from submissions made by literary journals across Canada, and, in recognition of the vital role journals play in discovering new writers, McClelland & Stewart makes its own award of $2,000 to the journal that has submitted the winning entry.

Last year McClelland & Stewart inaugurated another competition, with the Ontario College of Art's third-year design class, for the cover of *The Journey Prize Anthology*. The winning design this year is by Margaret So.

The Journey Prize Anthology has established itself as one of the most prestigious in the country. The anthology has become a who's who of up-and-coming writers, and many of the authors whose early work has appeared in the anthology's pages have gone on to single themselves out with collections of short stories and literary awards. The Journey Prize itself is the most significant monetary award given in Canada to a writer at the beginning of his or her career for a short story or excerpt from a longer fiction work in progress.

McClelland & Stewart would like to acknowledge the continuing enthusiastic support of writers, literary journal editors, and the public in the common celebration of the emergence of new voices in Canadian fiction.

Contents

MARY BORSKY

Maps of the Known World

When I was sixteen, my father brought home a man for me to marry. The man's name was Pete Paska and he sat down at the kitchen table without needing to be asked twice.

I was at the other end of the table, chewing the flavour out of a pack of gum, two or three sticks at a time, my history book open to a chapter called, "The Glory that was Greece."

"Such a man! Such a man!" my father said, grinning at my mother and me, but mostly at Pete Paska. "He can speak perfect English and perfect Ukrainian. Who's going to make Doreen a better husband than this?"

I stopped chewing when I heard my name.

My father's face was flushed and happy, and Pete Paska's face was a shiny birthday balloon. They brought the smell of snow and whisky into the house with them.

"He's got a good indoor job down there at the train station," my father said, pressing Pete Paska's shoulder. "He's a man for the future! He's a man for progress! He's a man for action!"

"See this salt-shaker?" Pete Paska asked loudly, pointing at the rabbit-shaped salt-shaker in the middle of the table. He had a forceful manner and I couldn't help but pay attention.

"Is this salt-shaker going to move by itself?" he demanded. He looked around at us, but didn't wait for anyone to answer. "No! It will not!" he said. "It moves when someone moves it!" Then he picked up the salt-shaker and held it dramatically over the table, giving us a minute to take this in.

My father grinned happily.

Doreen. Man. Husband. Future. I heard every word my father said.

I stared at Pete Paska from behind my bangs. I'd never seen him closer than across the street, or connected him with anything except, in a general sort of way, the train station.

He was an older man. Twenty-six or twenty-seven, maybe. He was shorter than my father, but more muscular. He had dark eyes, wavy black hair, and slightly yellowish, gnawed-down-looking teeth, the kind some small industrious animal might have, a beaver, say, or a muskrat. I got a good view of his teeth because he smiled at me every few minutes.

I looked up for a while, but then tried to go back to my homework. We were having a test and our teacher was known to ask trick questions, such as what was the name of Alexander the Great's horse.

"She's shy," my father said, as he placed two whisky glasses on the table, one in front of Pete Paska and one in front of himself.

"Still water runs deep," Pete Paska said, and smiled at me again.

My mother, her back a brick wall, kept washing dishes. She banged cups onto the shelf, clattered forks into the drawer, and slammed pots into the cupboard.

"*Di Bozheh!*" my father said, toasting Pete Paska, "To your health!" He held up his glass which had a donkey painted on it.

"*Di Bozheh!*" Pete Paska answered. His glass had a rooster on it.

"To the Old Country!"

"To the New Country!"

"To Family!"

"To Marriage!"

"To Progress!"

"To the Future!"

"To Action!"

"Why are you in all of a sudden such a hurry to marry her off?" my mother yelled the second Pete Paska shut the door behind him. "What's the big rush? She's got lots of time yet to get married!"

"He counts for something in this town," my father said, still happy from the good time he'd had with Pete Paska. "He's a Big Wheel down there at the train station. Four guys working for him and it's all the time, 'Yes, Pete! No, Pete! Anything you say, Pete!'"

"What about school?" my mother countered. "Shouldn't she at least finish school? Shouldn't she finish school and work for a while like the other girls?"

"You think men like Pete Paska grow like mushrooms after the rain?"

My mother swept the floor and scooped the dust into the wood stove which sat alongside the newer gas range.

"At least let her finish this year," she said, clinking the round lid back onto the wood stove. "At least let her finish grade eleven."

I heard the bedsprings creak in my parents' bedroom off the kitchen. I knew my father was sitting down to take his shoes off.

"You think she's better off with one of those Jailbird-Johannsens?" he called out. "Or maybe that shiftless Bert Strain? People like you, they never know when they got it good." The bedsprings creaked again. "Perfect English! And perfect Ukrainian!"

As I rested my head and arms on the table, I noticed I hardly breathed. I hardly had to. This wasn't new, though. Sometimes I could go for long periods, hardly breathing at all. At school we learned about evolution and how fish climbed out of the ocean and developed lungs. Something like that was happening to me too, I thought, though in my case it was going one step further. In my case, it felt as though I was gradually getting to the point where I didn't need to breathe at all. It didn't seem strange though, no more so than other things that happened, growing pains in my legs, or cramps before my period.

When I went to bed, I found I could hardly shut my eyes. There were two places. This place, this shadowy, half-secret, hard-to-breathe-in world of home, and the other place, the fast-paced, too-bright world of school, homework, tests, who-said-what, who-likes-who, the Valentine's Dance.

I flipped my pillow over and ran through the times tables which had always put me to sleep before. In the distance I could hear the trains – Pete Paska's trains – call out to one another. I imagined them racing past the things we'd drawn on maps at school – black pencil-crayoned oil derricks, golden sheaves of wheat, apple orchards, smoky factories, cities whose names we'd had to copy from the atlas, and fish emblazoned on the blue and wavy sea.

The next morning, when I went to the kitchen, my mother was stirring the porridge and crying.

"When I got married," she said, "I thought, poor man, he needs a woman to cook and clean for him. I thought washing his clothes was all I had to do." She blew her nose and turned, embarrassed but stubborn, to look at me. "There's more to it than that, though. A man expects more. Did you know that?"

A mouthful of scalding tea stopped at the top of my throat. I stood up, managed to swallow, then placed my cup on the table. My mother followed me as I got my homework, zipped it into my binder, put on my parka and boots.

"You know about that, don't you?" she asked as I opened the door to leave. "You know what happens, don't you?"

I rushed out into the stinging cold, my cheeks burning, my plastic binder stiff in my hands. I put my head down into the wind and walked as fast as I could toward the school.

Terrible things could happen, I knew that. Take your average awful thing, multiply by four, and that was probably closer to the truth. Your car could get cut in two on the railroad tracks. You could get put in an iron lung. You could have your leg eaten off by a bear, like the new Pentecostal minister. Barely believable things happened between men and women in bed – somehow I wasn't totally surprised – then there was the business of childbirth, of being strapped to a delivery table, of screaming in pain, of possibly bleeding to death, see, I knew about that.

And what was that other terrible thing hovering behind me like a black dog just outside my field of vision? I stopped walking for a moment to let it take shape in my mind, and then rushed on. Oh yes, you could have Pete Paska, smiling and muskrat-toothed, waiting to marry you.

At school, we talked about the Valentine's Dance. Everyone was on a committee. I'd signed up for the decorating committee in a smaller sub-committee charged with the responsibility of making three hundred pink Kleenex flowers for the huge heart on stage.

Beverly Cox, Gwen Farris, Stacey Reed, and I sat in a circle of chairs in the over-heated typing room with ten boxes of pink Kleenex, and talked about who was going with who to the dance. Beverly and Stacey had definitely been asked, Gwen had sort of been asked, and I was pretty sure I was about to be asked. Bryce Bliss had turned around in Math class to help me with my Math for two days in a row, and I thought it highly possible that he would ask me. As far as I knew, he hadn't asked anyone else.

None of the four of us had new dresses for the dance, but as we pleated and fluffed the pink Kleenex, we agreed unanimously that new clothes were not what counted. What counted was a girl's personality. After all, it wasn't as if this was our wedding day. For our weddings, naturally we planned to go whole hog.

For our weddings we would have to choose between taffeta, satin, *peau de soie*, and white velvet. We would be forced to consider whether our veils would be cocktail length, chapel length, or ankle length. Would our necklines be high or low? Would our sleeves be lily-pointed or short and worn with long white gloves?

Gwen told us that the red-haired girl at the telephone office had just married, not in a wedding gown, but in an ordinary good dress. "It makes sense," Gwen pointed out. "Why not buy a dress you'll be able to wear again and again?"

Although the talk of wedding gowns made me nervous, I voted against economizing in this way.

"After all," I pointed out, "a girl needs something to look forward to besides just doing the man's laundry and so forth."

"Doreen always makes sex sound so awful," Stacey Reed said with a superior smile. "I don't think sex is awful. I think sex is beautiful, like a painting of a sunset, or classical music."

Classical? I thought with alarm. *Classical?* I liked Hawaiian.

"No worse than a hog through a chute," said Beverly Cox, who lived on a farm.

"Horses do it," someone said. "Cows. Pigs."

"Earthworms."

"No, stupid," the others said.

I dumped the Kleenex flowers on the floor. "What number are we up to?" I asked. "I better count them."

"What's wrong, Doreen?" Stacey laughed. "You look ready to faint. You're afraid of all that, aren't you? I bet you are. I bet you're scared stiff of your wedding night."

"Yes," I said, losing count. "I mean, no." The girls laughed again.

We glued the Kleenex flowers onto a huge heart-shaped sheet of cardboard we'd pieced together from boxes.

On the intercom, the principal said that the Valentine's Dance was in grave danger of being cancelled if students failed to apply themselves more diligently to the curriculum as laid out by the Ministry.

At the end of the day, the grade eleven students were called back to the History room because of the poor results of the History test. Apparently some answers had been scrawled indifferently in pencil. Other papers had been handed in under false names. Jokes had been offered in response to the question: Describe the principle that Archimedes discovered in his bath.

The class was given a penalty assignment which was to be copied from the board. The teacher, however, made an exception for five students who had, he said, approached the test in a mature manner. The list was read aloud and I was one of them.

As the five of us picked up our books and left the room, Bryce Bliss – the boy I'd hoped would ask me to the dance – looked up with blanket contempt, and called after us, "Hens!"

At home I ground graham crackers, corn syrup, and condensed milk into a mash and ate it from the mixing bowl. Then I went to my bedroom and lay down on the covers.

I woke when my mother pushed open my bedroom door.

"He's here," she said. "He wants to see you." It was dark and the light from the kitchen shone behind her so I couldn't see her face.

"Who's here?"

"Pete Paska."

"Pete Paska? What does he want me for?"

My mother looked back toward the kitchen and rubbed her fingertips on the bib of her apron.

"Tell him I'm in bed."

"In bed? But it's only seven."

"Tell him I'm not here."

"How am I supposed to say that?" she hissed. "He knows you're here. Just talk to him. It's not going to kill you just to talk to him."

I felt my forehead for fever, then finally stood up and went to the kitchen. I felt like I'd eaten a tin can.

Pete Paska was spreading income tax forms and an open ledger on the table. He stepped back to check the all-over effect, then looked up at me and smiled.

"A thief hides a crust of bread, but an honest man hides nothing!" he said. "Come. Let's get your Dad."

My mother frowned and rubbed her hand on her forehead, but handed me my parka and boots.

Pete Paska's car, still idling at the front of the house, was hot and smelled of over-sweet perfume from the tree-shaped air-freshener that hung on the rearview mirror. He adjusted various dials, fans, and mirrors. I sat with my shoulder pressed against the side door and tried to block the scent of the air-freshener by breathing as little as possible.

I expected to drive straight downtown to get my Dad, but I could see Pete Paska was looping around the other way, taking the scenic route. We drove past Ed Ferleyko's Garage, past The Pearly Gates Motel, past the Ukrainian church, then approached the school where there were already lights on in readiness for the Valentine's Dance.

I breathed in a strangulated way because of the air-freshener. What was happening? Where was I headed? I was sixteen, but it seemed as if my life had dissolved into the night. What lay ahead? Nothing but cooking and cleaning, plus the other things men expected in addition.

"Life is for the living," Pete Paska observed energetically. I could feel the force of his smile through the hot perfumey air of the car.

"I have to throw up," I said.

Pete Paska pulled over immediately.

I got out, grateful to be near the school, and ran to the boys' washroom on the main floor. But I couldn't relax with the tall white urinals looming up like tombstones behind me. And besides, now that I was away from the air-freshener, I felt better. I decided to go upstairs to the girls' washroom.

Upstairs, the lights were off, except for the typing room, where the huge Kleenex heart was still drying on the floor. Someone had left the window open and snow had blown in on one side of the heart. I tried to dust the snow off, but some of it had already melted, and the heart was soggy on one side.

I pulled the cushioned teacher's chair over to the open window, and leaned back, letting the blowing snow melt on my face. I reached onto the roof that extended below the window and made several small snowballs which I ate slowly, one at a time.

On the window ledge, there was a textbook someone had left open to a picture. *Ptolemy draws a map of the known world*, the caption said.

The picture showed a handsome man in bathrobe-type clothes. He was drawing at a table, while four other men looked on, admiring.

When I looked at the picture, I felt a dull weight behind my eyes. How could this man be so public? So sure of himself? Could it really be so easy? Weren't there people in those days who said, "Don't do that – be careful – you've got it wrong"?

I was still trying to figure this out when I heard heavy footsteps in the hall. I jumped up to move the chair back, but the person almost instantly appeared in the doorway.

It was Pete Paska.

"I've been waiting," he said. His outline was as clear as if it'd been drawn with India ink. He was no longer smiling.

"This is getting wrecked here," I said, pointing to the heart. He didn't say anything.

"Could you do just one thing?" I said. "Could you take it downstairs to the gym?"

"What good is this?" he said, and stared at me for a moment. "This is for kids." But he picked it up.

"Turn right at the bottom, then left," I said, watching as he started to manoeuvre the slightly soggy heart downstairs. "I'll just be a minute. Maybe two."

I needed at least that long to kill myself.

There was a stapler on the desk – too small, I thought. There was a large guillotine-style paper-cutter on a table – too big, I told myself. Then I looked at the open window and stepped out onto the roof. This was just right, I thought, and felt pleased with my own little joke.

I'd been here before, though never in winter. Sometimes in spring, I climbed out here with a few other girls to eat lunch and scratch our initials into the hot tar on the roof. One girl – Jeanette Tremblay – pulled off pieces of the tar which she chewed like gum, but I was never able to develop a taste for it.

I waded through the snow to the edge of the roof and looked down. It was further down than I remembered. There were two tar barrels directly below where I was, so I moved along the edge of the roof until there was nothing but the flat snowy schoolyard beneath me.

This was the exact spot where we'd built a snow fort in grade five, boys against the girls, which had been so much simpler. There was the flagpole where Ollie Stout had frozen his tongue, just beyond, the road I walked to school everyday. Nearby, I could see the shadows of the willows along the river where I swam in summer, worrying that my mother would kill me if I drowned.

The snowflakes were big and slow now. In the distance, I could make out my own house, with its tiny yellow kitchen window and snow blanketing the roof, as pretty from where I stood as a house on a Christmas card. In the other direction, I could even make out the dark shape of the hospital where I'd been born. I felt like a ghost looking out over my own life. I felt fine.

Behind me, the lights in the typing room went off, then on again.

"No one's here," I heard someone say.

Then Pete Paska said my name.

I held my breath and jumped.

There was a flash of light, but no sound. I folded silently like a Monopoly board. Then there was nothing.

After some time, I felt a burning pain in my arm and shoulder, but tried to ignore it. Snow started to melt and trickle down the back of my neck. I shifted my head, one arm, then the other. Finally, I stood up and dusted myself off.

From where I stood, I could see Pete Paska's car still idling in front, the headlights catching on the falling snow. And beyond that were two or three cars pulling into the parking lot at the far end of the yard.

I turned in the dark snowy playground, and walked the opposite way, in the direction of downtown. When I came to the lighted window of the laundromat, I opened the door and went in to warm up.

But it was different from the last time I was here. The rows of washing machines were gone. There were only orange chairs along one wall, and a canvas mailbag and cardboard boxes along the other side. Maxine Jack, with her dyed hair and her police dog, was behind the counter. Maxine Jack and her police dog meant this was the new Bus Depot. The police dog looked at me and rumbled, but stayed where it was.

I sat down on one of the orange vinyl chairs. The room still smelled of bleach and soap. On the wall there was a bus schedule that had been kissed here and there with lip-sticked lips. I was shaky, and my left arm and shoulder still burned.

Beside me, someone lit a cigarette, then held the open pack out to me. He was a tall man in a black cowboy hat.

When I reached for a cigarette, I found my hand shaking so much I had to steady it with my other one. My left arm hurt when I moved it, but I lifted it again to steady my wrist when the man lit my cigarette.

I pulled on the smoke, then breathed it out. My eyes watered and my lungs felt hot, but I was determined not to choke.

Outside, a car streaked past, travelling much too fast for the roads. I looked out, but only saw red tail lights receding into the storm.

I could feel the man in the black cowboy hat watching me.

"You always shake like that?" he asked.

I held out my almost fluttering hands, and watched them a moment, surprised by them myself.

"I'll get over it," I said.

I pulled the smoke into my lungs and pushed it out. Pulled it in, pushed it out.

"Inhale," I told myself. "Exhale. Inhale, exhale."

It was warm and, for the moment, peaceful here. I decided not to think about what I was going to do next.

I sat on the orange chair. I breathed in and out. I watched the cigarette smoke curl up like roads to the north, south, east, and west of me.

GABRIELLA GOLIGER

Song of Ascent

 In Jerusalem we lived on a roof.

"A view to die for," my mother said.

"An inferno. *Gehenna*," my father said. "And dangerous too."

He was thinking not just of the months in 1948 when the shells rained down and the streets shook with explosions, but afterwards when snipers still took pot-shots from the Old City walls. But it was the only place my parents could find in those years, what with many buildings still bombed-out craters and the city divided down the middle by a jagged line of barbed wire fences and walls.

Although winters were cold and wet in Jerusalem and a bitter wind raged around the walls of our little house, my parents both remember the baking sun best, the eternal cloudless day that lasted from May to October. In their stories and arguments it was always summer.

It was not exactly a house we lived in. An addition rather, an afterthought. A simple whitewashed block of concrete and plaster – two rooms and a galley kitchen – perched on a broad flat roof of a three-storey apartment building. It had been built, like many others just like it, in answer to the stream of immigrants and refugees pouring into the country in the 1930s. Self-contained, it sat amid the water tanks, rusting bedframes and odds and ends dumped there temporarily by other tenants. A few feet away was our connection with the outside world, a door that led to the long, steep stairwell of the main building. No one standing on Eden Street down below could have guessed at our existence.

Seated on her stool in front of the door, with a bowl of potatoes for scraping in her lap, my mother could see clear across the city, to other shacks on other roofs, to the domes, crosses, towers, and the thick Crusade-era walls of the Old City where the Jordanian sentries stood. She could even see the Arab women's clothes-lines strung along their roof-tops, their sheets and *keffiyehs* stiffening in the sun.

Her view. Her roof. Fierce hot to a bare-soled foot, seared by the relentless blaze from nine in the morning until five in the afternoon. Her plaza to walk about in, to wash clothes in before she hoisted me and my basket in her arms and headed off to clean houses in Rehavia.

"The sunsets over Jerusalem," she later told me with a quaver in her voice. "The flowers." Spring anemones like tiny flames in the scrub fields between neighbourhoods.

"What about the flies? Hey?" my father would say. He would tell about a pan of hummus he'd seen in the market, blackened with a solid layer of flies that leapt momentarily out of the way when the bearded vendor dipped his cup into the paste, and resettled to their feast an instant later.

Jerusalem of gold, Jerusalem of dust. Over the years, I became used to the two sets of stories and adept at braiding them together into complementary strands. Even today when I wake, terrified, from an old dream in which I dangle by a thread over a gaping void, I listen in my mind for my parents' voices, speaking one on top of the other. I weave and weave their warring words into a net that holds us together and safe.

Every day at noon my father used to lug himself home from his job at the import company for lunch and siesta. He trudged through crowded, clamorous streets, along fiery pavements, across roads gummy with half-melted asphalt and through air heavy with smells of cheap petrol, rotting vegetables, and beggars' spit. He arrived limp and drained at our building's stairwell, which was sweetly cool and dark on the first floor, warmer and brighter as he rose. Finally, he thrust his head into the white-hot glare, shielding his eyes against those extra torments, spears of light that glinted off metal flashings and wash buckets.

If I was at play with my spoon and pail under the tin awning over the front door, he swooped me up and swung me around. He held me like a parcel high above his head, presenting me to the sky. But our moment of delight was short-lived. After a quick lunch, during which he chewed, without appetite, on his bread and butter and cheese, he staggered into the shuttered bedroom and rolled onto the bed. There was no point in my mother chatting about her employer Frau Doktor Mercaz, for instance, a woman who had an eagle eye for islands of dust on the legs of the dining-room table. He would shake his head as if trying to shake free of something thickening around him and close his eyes and drift down, down into the well of suffocating sleep.

My mother, standing by the dresser, would see his fingertips twitch and his chin jerk, a gesture that seemed, though she knew he was asleep, to deliberately dismiss her. She would stir about the room, restless, open a dresser drawer and close it with a snap; she would pick me up and wander to the front door and back while my head dropped against her shoulder. At last, she settled me in my crib, and sat down on the low wall that ran around the perimeter of the roof to look out over the city in the afternoon haze, the one time of the day when the streets fell silent. She would fill her nostrils with the hot, dry air which went down like a gulp of strong drink. The city – both sides – spread out before her, sun-scorched, salt-white. Her pulse throbbed with the dangerous heat. Another minute and she would have to go back to her chair under the awning.

Let him sleep, she told herself. Let him turn his face to the wall. Let Frau Doktor mutter into her herring tidbits about the clumsy, inefficient help. She stared more intently at the city, lost herself in the tiers of houses that spilled down valleys, the weathered stones and hills, dazzling, incandescent pillars of salt under her gaze. In the distance, the mountains of Judea danced watery shimmer, like part of the sky.

My father had never been able to get used to the Middle Eastern heat. His blood was European, nurtured for generations by the fresh mountain chill of Bohemia. Nothing could be more foreign than the stupefying heat of this ancestral homeland. Low blood pressure, the doctor had said with a shrug. There were plenty others like him. Bad luck. From the day he stepped off the boat, no, even before they reached shore, he'd felt a heaviness in his limbs and his eyelids, a clutching at his heart. From then on, for seventeen years, he fought the downward pull of drowsiness, and when he did sleep, day or night he awoke unrefreshed, head swimming. His ideals of a pioneering life dried up under the blistering sun. He'd planted orange trees, hacking at the stony ground with a short-handled hoe. Shovelful by shovelful, stone by stone. His youth flaked off and fell into the parched earth which he loosened, raked, and watered with the feeble, rubber-tainted stream from the irrigation hose. The work at the import company was easier. There were shutters and ceiling fans. Still, it was all he could do to keep his head from lolling forward onto his typewriter. One day he looked up from the clatter of keys and out the window at the feet that tramped along the sidewalk. All seemed eager and energetic, while he sat like the frog too boiled to leap. A few more years and it would be too late.

Canada. The word was like a spring released. He met a Mr. Samson from Montreal whose smooth, pink cheeks were a living advertisement for civilized climates, a startling contrast to the wrinkled, sun-ravaged faces of Jerusalemites. Samson promised a job in his travel agency. He also promised that, within a year, they would have their own house and garden. "That's how it is in Canada," he said, spreading plump palms in the air. My father didn't believe it about the house and garden, but even if the half of it were true, even a quarter, he told my mother, we would be better off. She crossed brown arms against her chest, her lips settled into a pout.

"Ha. You think everything will be golden. And if it doesn't work out? What will we do? Be stuck there with no one and nothing."

"Other people succeed. Why shouldn't I?"

"Other people fail too."

He saw her planted against him. Her face – once so soft and carefree – now a knot of reproach, counting up her disappointments over the years, hoarding them to shower down over his head. Still, one day he simply put it to her that he was leaving. She could make up her mind to come with him or stay behind. The choice was hers.

We arrived in Montreal on a sweltering day in August and, after finding a rooming-house, sat in Dominion Square amid a swarm of pigeons. My mother scratched at a vicious heat rash that bubbled up on her arms and legs, something she'd never had before. My father, head in his hands, willed away the panic in his chest. Senseless emotion. I gurgled and toddled after the pigeons.

A piece of newspaper in the waste-basket caught my mother's eye and she fished it out. She laboured over the headline. "Ha, ha." Fate was having its joke, so she would laugh. Why not. Ha, ha, ha. She would make him laugh too, make him admit that she was not so ignorant of the world after all. My father glanced at the headline she thrust into his face. "Record heatwave hits: over 95 in the shade." His gaze drifted past her to fix on the green-bronze statue of someone – neither of them recognized the name – in the middle of the square. He said nothing for a few moments so that she thought he wouldn't comment at all. Then, in a flat voice, "You think that would make the papers in Israel? Here it's an event."

After the rooming-house on Mansfield, we bunked in with the Fishbein's on Durocher, the Borscht Alley. Two families in a two-bedroom apartment. Yankle Fishbein's shitty diapers in a pail on the kitchen floor. The windows steamed up from boiling cabbage. My mother and father hardly saw each other those months. He worked from early morning to evening for Samson the Swindler while she worked in the apartment with the Fishbeins, all of them hunched over, with metal punches in their hands, pressing rhinestones into bracelets for five cents a dozen. Under-the-table money.

At the end of the winter, my father finally found us an apartment of our own in a no man's land of newly developed streets between two older neighbourhoods, one classy, the other poor. It was a decent enough apartment on a decent enough street, he thought. A park nearby and a school. The first rung in a long but reliable ladder that might one day even mean a cottage on a lake in the Laurentians like Samson had, Augusts spent with feet up on a deck chair in the shade of sweet-scented pines. Why not? My father showed my mother the features while the janitor, a man with a face as grey as his shirt, lounged against the wall outside the apartment door and smoked.

"Look at the size of the refrigerator," my father said. He ran a finger over the thick coat of frost under the freezer, and tested the coolness of the clean white walls.

"On the top floor, like you wanted. A balcony."

A balcony, indeed, she thought. It faced a lane way, a gravel parking lot, and the backs of other squat, three-storey buildings, all shoulder to shoulder like policemen on guard. The back door, as my father demonstrated, opened to a fire-escape that led to a narrow, enclosed courtyard.

"Here's where we put garbage," he said with a wave of his hand through the half-open door. He was about to close it again when my mother pushed past and stepped out onto the landing to survey the scene. A black metal stairway zigzagged downwards past other back doors and bathroom windows. She sniffed the courtyard smells – damp cement, coal dust, and garbage. Looking up, the sides of the building formed a chute with a rectangle of sky at the top. A breeze eddied some dead leaves around the gutters.

My father worked. While Samson drummed up business over lunch and cigars at the delicatessen, my father sat with the phone pressed against his cheek and his hands busy with file cards and schedules.

The travel business, as my father later explained to me, was about creating connections, a bridge of good faith that could span miles and bureaucracies, safely delivering a Mrs. Seligman of Côte des Neiges Street, first to the shops of London and Paris, and finally to a happy reunion with her husband waiting in Rome.

"Absolutely, Mrs. Seligman," my father chanted into the telephone while he jotted notes on file cards. "May 15 departure . . ."

Directories consulted. Schedules and prices compared. Calls

to the airline and steamship line made to double check. More calls and consultations with Mrs. Seligman. Flights booked. Dates changed. More calls to Mrs. Seligman and to the airline. Deposits delivered. Passport application filed. Hotel in London cabled. Collect call from Rome accepted. Pension in Paris confirmed. Porter promised. Airline ticket collected. (A run at noontime ten blocks down St. Catherine Street to the company's office on Beaver Hall Hill, and back again.)

One more phone call. Person-to-person from a growly Mr. Seligman in Naples. "Tell her not to come. She is not to come." Reservations, connections, confirmations, deposits, applications – the bridge collapsed. Everything, including my father's meagre commission, cancelled.

My father could only sigh, replace the receiver in its cradle, tear up the Seligman file cards, busy himself with another file, and wait for the phone to ring again.

My mother could not at first understand why she found our street so forbidding. It was the lack of trees, she finally realized. There were only saplings on small squares of lawn in front of each house. Weak, pathetic things dwarfed by the massive brick behind and the wide road in front. The houses had a sameness to them, like soldiers' tombstones, but it was the treeless nakedness that was most disturbing. It was worst on the bright May days that now arrived and exposed the graceless lines of unadorned doorways and windows and monotonous brick.

Pleased to have discovered a fact, she felt compelled to state it out loud. "This is Canada," she said to my father. "Wild forest everywhere, but on our street, only twigs."

His voice poured over her like coarse sand with fierce cutting edges. "You don't like it, go back. I'll buy you a ticket. Sea or air, your choice."

"Why do you hate me? What have I done to you!"

He turned and pulled away to his side of the bed. There he lay, rigid and self-contained, and she knew he would be able to lie like that, neat as a board, without flinging a careless arm or leg towards her side all night long. To throw her arms around him now would be to smash like an egg on concrete. Still, she couldn't bring herself to move away to the couch. She hung onto the bedsheets, twisting and twisting the sweat-dampened cloth in her hands.

One of the first things that my father bought with the few dollars he managed to set aside, after all the weekly and monthly expenses had been paid, was a vacuum cleaner. Riding the streetcar home that evening, he stood with one proud arm draped around a tall cardboard box stamped "Morgan's Department Store." Canister, hoses, attachments, and cord emerged from the cardboard package that he unwrapped while my mother watched from the doorway of the living room.

"I don't need this thing," she said.

"It will make your life easier. Look." He plugged the vacuum cleaner in, scattered some shreds of toilet paper on the carpet and proceeded to demonstrate, just as the salesman had at the store. The motor still whining, he offered the hose to my mother. She shuffled across the carpet slowly, reached out her hand. Crack. A shock. Or so she said. The sucking mouth then stuck to the carpet.

"Glide the hose. Don't rub. Don't drag so hard."

My mother jerked forward and the canister flipped over on its back, making the motor whine louder and higher, like a scream of alarm.

"You'll get used to it," he said. But except when my father himself took it out on Saturdays, the vacuum cleaner stood abandoned in the closet.

My mother worked. She attacked the kitchen floor with a string mop and a pail of sudsy water. She slapped the mop around the linoleum as she had never done in Jerusalem, with a violent energy. She dipped, wrung, slapped, and scrubbed some more, sending streams of grey water into the cracks of the linoleum and under the cabinets to swell the crumbs and lumps that had collected there. She hoisted the metal pail, marched it to the toilet and tipped it in, listening with satisfaction to the splash and digestive gurgle. On her knees, leaning over the bathtub, she scrubbed the bedsheets between her knuckles. She rubbed, squeezed, twisted, wrung, then heaved the wash-tub to her hip and marched it to the clothes-line.

She attacked the living-room rug, the only one in the house, first with a stiff brush, then with a damp cloth, dabbing and picking at the lint. She would have preferred to drag the carpet to the balcony railing and beat the dust out with a stick. Heavy work and dirty, but effective. But people didn't do that in Canada. Could she imagine the names we'd get called, said my father, if the neighbours below saw clouds of dust flying around their windows and clothes-line? Let alone what the landlord would say.

My father noticed lint on the living-room carpet, and worse, crumbs, shreds of vegetables, and indefinable grime peeking out from under the kitchen cabinets. In Jerusalem, unwiped crumbs produced an instant parade of red ants that poured out from a crack in the wall. Also cockroaches. He remembered his nausea, stumbling into the kitchen for a glass of water at night and finding the scrabbling bodies, the evil shine of their brown-black shells in the electric light. Here dirt had no such drastic consequences. Maybe that was why she let it pile up. No, he reminded himself, it was not deliberate. She was like a dreamy, awkward child, mooning about, refusing to focus on things right in front of her nose. He knew better by now than to complain. But one day, while she was out of the room, he took the broom to the litter under the kitchen cabinets. A mistake. He should have waited until she was out of the house altogether. She stormed into the kitchen like a maddened hen.

"What are you doing? What are you trying to prove?"

"I'm helping you. Is that a crime?"

"I've already swept."

"Well, you missed a little bit." He pointed with the dustpan at the spot he'd been working on. He spoke in the most innocent, good-natured tone he could muster, but a guilty smile crept over his face. There was something else he wanted to say, and now he'd forgotten. How could she make him feel guilty for sweeping?

"You try to humiliate me. You want to tramp me down into the mud."

In her eyes, a poison was rising, a fevered glaze staring at him but seeing god-knows-what. She swallowed, took a deep breath and began to rage, calling him names, old woman, scorpion, snake, working herself up. All the while her voice rose higher, the glaze in her eyes became thicker, any moment, he knew, she would be over the edge, beyond all reasoning. He searched for calm words but there was nothing inside. Empty. And he could not erase the grin that settled on his face.

"So? Better a scorpion in the kitchen than cockroaches, don't you think?"

Her mouth fell open, not understanding. He pointed to under the cabinets.

"Soon the cockroaches will come to dinner, just like old times."

She flailed her fists at him so that he had to dodge around the kitchen with his arm raised to his face.

"Set the table for them," he giggled between his fingers. "Our honoured guests."

She slumped to the floor and cried, first in silent spasmodic sobs, next bawling, and finally screaming between clenched teeth, shrill, fiendish. She bit at her arm, dug into her legs with her nails. He saw red welts rise up on her skin and long red scratches that made his stomach lurch. His hands flew up to his eyes. A moment later he found what he'd been looking for: his anger, his sense of being the one who was wounded.

"Quiet. Get a hold of yourself." He stooped over her, grabbed her hands in a vise grip. "Remember the child for god's sake." I was in my bed, in the little room far away at the back of the apartment, but I'd been wakened by less of a racket before.

"I forbid this behaviour." He shook and shook until her cries subsided into a quiet keening, her head on her knees, rocking, unearthly strangled screams. Sickened, his own knees weak, he loosened his grip and stood up. When she finally raised her head to see what he was doing, she found him gone. He had left the room.

On his way to the bathroom to get ready for bed, my father noticed that the back door was ajar. He was about to lock it when he heard a sound, the rattle of metal, above his head. He stepped onto the landing and the breath froze in his throat. Someone was climbing up the short ladder that hung over the courtyard and led from the landing to the roof. My mother, in her bare feet and night-gown. To get onto the ladder, she would have had to clamber onto the narrow railing that surrounded our landing, then step sideways to the first rung. Now she was hoisting herself upwards with unhurried, deliberate motions while my father watched in silence. In a moment she was on the roof looking down the long chute of brick into the gloom below. Somewhere down there a bathroom light was on, illuminating a sharp elbow of zigzag railing on the second floor, but beyond that it was all black.

My father's voice finally came unstuck. "What are you doing?" he said softly, afraid to startle her. She didn't seem to hear. She stood there hugging herself and looking down while her night-gown fluttered against her legs in the wind. Although it was May, it was a frosty night, damp and windy. My father, dressed only in his undershirt and shorts, could sense, though he couldn't see, the thick bank of clouds rolling across the sky.

He cleared his throat.

"Hannah, get down from there."

She seemed lost in a trance of downward staring. He wasn't sure if she deliberately ignored him or really didn't hear. She swayed a little, arms tight to her chest.

"Hannah, please."

She didn't lift her head, and he stood motionless for a few moments, but in his mind he went over the steps he was about to take. A swift and noiseless leap up the ladder before she could notice, a firm grab around the waist, and, once he had her, he'd figure out from there how to get her down.

Apparently, at that very instant, I began to cry. The sound of my wailing, thin and distant, drifted up the corridor and out the open back door. I must have woken from a nightmare and was sobbing my fears to the walls around me. My mother looked up, startled and anxious.

"Go to her," she whispered.

"You go."

I continued to cry, frightened more than anything perhaps, by the dead quiet in the wall that lay between me and my parents' room. No sounds of the radio or voices or the clump of feet.

So my mother went around to where the ladder was, crouched, and put her bare feet back on the rungs. It was only half-way down that she realized what she was doing, where she was. She was suspended over nothingness, empty space that could just as well have been a chasm as vast and deep as the world itself in its power to swallow and annihilate her. Nothing separated her from the downward pull except cold metal rungs turning damp in her grip.

"Come down," she heard my father say. From the corner of her eye she saw the white of his undershirt below her on the landing. She couldn't move, she couldn't breathe. To loosen a muscle meant to lose all hold. Frozen in a crouch, her back bent double and aching. Nothing between her and a brutal smash but fingers locked to metal. Beneath her the ladder began to tremble against the brick. A relentless clatter.

"Come on, just a few more steps," my father pleaded.

In the meantime I was howling, louder and angrier, in my room alone. I was accustomed to someone coming in right away. Most likely I wanted to step out of my bed, run out of my room and find them, but was afraid of the pool of darkness around me, the stillness that lay thick and heavy in the rooms beyond.

"Take it easy. Don't panic," my mother heard my father say from a great distance. He moved closer into her line of vision and she saw with startling clarity how long and skinny his legs looked sticking out of his undershorts. Stork legs. She had a wild thought. "When this is over, I'll remember his legs and laugh."

A yank, a wrench of such force came now, she could not resist. Besides, her hands had already loosened. Her arms flew out into the empty air above her, her body, stone-heavy, rushed down. She crashed on top of him and on top of the metal garbage bin which flew off the landing, first the lid, then the rest of it, bouncing against three flights of fire-escape with hollow bangs. Beneath her, his arms both clung and lay pinned against her waist and his foot lay twisted between the landing railings. Slowly she rolled off him, and they both sat, stunned. He had a split lip and a sprained ankle; she, long gashes on her face where it had grazed against brick, massive bruises on one arm and an egg-sized lump on her forehead.

Hearing the merry clang of the trash can, the sound of doors and windows opening, and voices in the courtyard, I immediately stopped my crying. Calm and attentive, I waited for them to come.

SHAENA LAMBERT

The Falling Woman

Some of my dreams feel like memories. In one, Mother has cornered me in a stall. She is trying to get me to close my teeth over the snaffle bit. But it's massive in my mouth, it tastes like tin and the green spit of horses, if it is pushed over my tongue I will gag. Her hands are as fierce as weasel's claws, and they are tugging at the sides of my mouth.

In another I am bareback on Douna, her quarter-horse, while Mother is below and behind me, I can see the shadow of her black hat. The dry hills rise around us, pulsing with crickets. Then Mother slaps Douna's rump, and yells *grip*, but I can't grip, I can only bounce on my crotch in the white sunlight, watching the dirt blur while I tip away and fall.

Once Ben and I were lying here staring at the dark ceiling, and he asked me about my childhood. I grew up in the Okanagan Valley. It was dry, I said. There were cactuses about the size of your thumb bunched around the grey rocks. Hidden punishments. Tell me about your mother, he said. I changed the subject.

I don't talk about her. I dream her. As I walk along the slushy street, or heat my plastic dish of Stouffer's Veal Parmigiana in the microwave, I see the hills rising up, leached of colour, speckled by pines. Sauble Mountain curves above the flats like a reclining hip, a granite cliff cut into it, revealing the etched outline of a falling woman. It is hard to see her, it always was, you have to focus or have someone else point her out, and even then she is partly wishful. Her hair is five milky fissures. Her arching body is a scar in the rock, like a pock on the moon's face. She fled

25

a marriage her father had arranged – according to an Okanagan legend – galloping in the dark up the back of the mountain. But as she reached the top, the moon disappeared; she lost her way and plunged off the cliff.

I see Mother's legs, bowed from riding, her jeans tucked into her steel-toed boots, her checkered shirt which must have belonged to my grandfather – *Papa*. I see her belt with the cattle horns engraved on the buckle; they meet in the middle like a crescent moon. I see Mother's arthritic knuckles, her thumbs strong as crowbars. She rolls up her sleeve and throws down her hand, thumb up, on the kitchen table, daring Uncle Nesbit to a thumb wrestle. I see her walking out into the dirt yard, the screen door slapping behind her. She walks low in her hips because they ache, still, from my uncompromising birth – the only thing that was bigger than she was – the only thing that knocked her sideways, got her thumb down and twisted until she screamed.

All day today I couldn't picture her face; it blurred under her hat brim. Then I closed my eyes to sleep and her stare burnt into me, her mouth curled. I could see her gold incisor, the yellowed skin of her throat. *Ellen*, she screamed and I sat up in bed, *What the hell do you think you're doing?* Nothing, I wanted to say. I wanted to hold out my hands, show I hadn't touched myself. Then I remembered, she's dead. Any voices I hear come from me.

But now I can't fall back to sleep. I'll pay for it tomorrow. I'll be lightheaded as I clean teeth with my little tools, the tiny scaler, the suction hose, the miniature bowls that hold the prophy gel. This kind of work is like playing Barbie – everything's tiny, even the teeth reflected in the mirror.

Today I picked out parsley from the back fissures, then I poked my head into Dr. Stephen French's office. He had X-rays of an impacted wisdom tooth spread on his desk, the photograph of his wife and twin sons on the wall behind him. He looked up, startled, his eyes rimmed by round glasses, like dark birds caught for a moment in a trap. Then he followed me down the hall and we studied the patient together, under the heated lamp. When I passed Dr. French the silver amalgam I saw a mole near his collar.

One of these days I may close his office door behind me. *Look at this strange occlusion*, he will say, and I will stand behind him, observing the ghostly markings of teeth. Then I will touch that mole with my finger. He will close his eyes and shudder like a horse.

I never knew my father. When I was six, Serena, my cousin from Vancouver, told me I'd been born out of wedlock with a hired man. I'd seen Mother demonstrate a headlock on Walt, our current hired man: he'd stood stock still like a rabbit and remonstrated softly, *Now really, Mary*, before landing on his back on the floor. When Serena mocked me that day I knew Mother had done something unseemly, like the headlock on Walt, that had made my father want to disappear.

It was only when I was twelve that I got the facts from Aunt Clara, Serena's mother. That was the summer they drove into the dirt turn-around in a red convertible, chrome fenders and spokes and white vinyl top all shining at once. Serena sat proudly in the front, dressed in red-and-white seersucker, and when she stepped out carefully, so as not to dirty the white leather on her saddle shoes, I saw her dress had a magnificent bow at the back. I instantly wanted it. I wanted everything Serena had with a complete, black need the minute I saw it.

That night after supper I had Clara to myself. Serena had begged off the dishes, saying she was sick – but I knew she was soaking in the bath water reading the Signet Romance which she'd shown to me furtively that afternoon. Mother had gone to check on Douna's foal. As her lantern disappeared into the barn, Clara sighed. "Your mother used to follow Papa out there every night. They were inseparable." She had told me this story – it wasn't the one that interested me – about how, by age three, Papa had given my mother her first horse – not a pony, a gelding named Gibraltar. How Mother knew how to ride deep in her stirrups, cueing with the pressure of her legs. I remembered this story every time I circled Mother in the corral and she yelled, *Don't tiptoe, don't slump, don't flap your elbows, let out your lead when you canter.* I had two red ribbons hanging from the feed room wall, among the sea of her blue ones.

"What was my father like?" I asked.

Clara scrubbed at a casserole dish, her forearms swaying. He had a thin face and dark hair, she said, and he could blow smoke rings just by snapping his jaw. He sounded like the men at Dan's, the main bar in Keremeos. As we hurried by the open door one day, my mother's boots clumping on the board walk, I had glimpsed a man rubbing his white stomach, the eyes of other men glinting near the pool table. I couldn't picture my mother succumbing to any man, but her particular disgust at the men who visited Dan's – the way she gripped my hand, then yanked it as laughter rolled out of the darkness – made it harder to imagine.

"I think she did it to rebel against Papa," Clara said, scouring at the glass casserole beneath the filmy water. "But it back-fired. When Papa found out, he swore he'd horsewhip Les if he didn't marry her – and horsewhip your mother if she didn't agree."

Clara stopped and looked out toward the barn. We could see Mother's light through the feed-room window.

"Then Papa had his stroke, out in the field. After he was buried, your Mother told Les to get going. Get going or she'd run him off."

"But why?"

"That's your Mother," Clara shook her head. "I guess she couldn't stand the thought of having him around one more second." She pulled out the plug and let the brownish water drain away.

After Mother died I found an old picture of her at the bottom of the horse medicine cupboard. She is about fourteen, standing on the back of Gibraltar, holding the reins like a circus performer, smiling brazenly into the camera. I could see the defiant beginning of anger – of wanting to be a boy, being told she should have been a boy – and being wrapped up in a girl's body. I imagine her crossing the bare yard to the horse barn in the afternoon sun, her shadow elongated in the dirt. She pushes her new breasts in with her elbows so she will not see them in her shadow. She is fiercely repelled by the growth of her body – for good reason. It will prove fertile as a chicken's egg. It will betray her.

My heels ache from a day squeezed in high heeled slip-ons. I wouldn't be caught dead in orthopedics; that would be the beginning of the end, the spiral toward old age, which starts with orthopedic shoes, moves to opaque stockings, then spreads up to swallow hips, back, and finally hair. The last stage is when the scalp shows beneath the dyed strands of henna. Then it's death – the body lies back and comes apart, only the bones and teeth are left, gleaming against the soil.

It was two months ago this weekend that Ben and I drove to his sister's cottage on Lake Huron. We arrived at night and made love in darkness. As I tried to sleep – tossing in the strange bed – the wind threw sand at the kitchen window. Next morning I saw the whitewashed shingles had blown away in chunks, leaving gaps of tar-paper.

I walked to the beach and let the wind hit me. When I came back, I found Ben around the side, out of the wind, chopping driftwood into splinters. He held on to the wood for too long, then brought the axe down and almost nipped off his fingers.

"I need to talk to you," he said.

We squatted next to the house, looking out at the garden of driftwood, listening to the wind moaning against the boards.

"I've been in agony." The words came out with his hot breath. "I've decided to tell Judy – maybe she'll take me back, maybe she won't, but I have to come clean."

On the drive home I sat beside him, not saying a word, drinking coffee from my styrofoam cup, drawing lines in it with my thumbnail. Ben had taken a shower before we left and his hair was wet, even his nose shone. "I have a lot to thank you for," he said. I peeled away a bit of cuticle and left a pink crescent beside my thumbnail.

Now I yank the blinds down, they rattle to the radiator, and when I turn the plastic wand there is darkness. Back in bed I ease my legs out, leaning on one hip, trying to find the position that will let me sleep.

All day Serena and I had been planning to go to the stable to read her paperback. But in the morning we changed the horse sprinklers, then drove with Mother and Clara into town. It was late afternoon when I slid the stable door open on its runner, closing it behind Serena. Inside, the clay floor retained its coolness, and I could hear Douna blowing through her nose. Mother's collection of tack hung on the walls around us – bridles with bits dangling down, reins coiled around each other, western saddles splayed on their racks.

We hoisted ourselves onto the wall between two stalls and sat with our legs dangling down, watching the colt nurse from Douna's swollen teat. Serena took a frosted lipstick from her red purse.

"Put some on," she offered.

"I can't." I said. "My mother will see."

"What's she going to do? Whip you?" She made a shiver of feminine contempt – for my mother for whipping me, for me for being whipped. Then she reached into her purse again, drawing out, at last, the dog-eared paperback – *My Darling Ravager!* On the front a pirate captain, his shirt streaming open at the chest, clenched the hilt of his sword with one hand, while his other grasped a woman by the waist. Her back was arched, her lips open and her eyes closed. "Swooning with desire," Serena explained. She leafed to a place she had marked.

"This is the part where the pirate captain has tied Lady Birkwith in the hold. Listen to this: *'You swine,' she cried out, her violet eyes flashing, 'you'll pay for this.' He gave her a mocking half-smile, then she felt his strong arms grip her. She breathed in his murky scent, gasping as his mouth found hers. She tried to struggle, but found she could not, did not want to. A hot tide of passion surged through her. Then she gasped again, as the sweet torture of his hands began to unlace the bodice of her gown.*"

We looked at each other and laughed.

"How big are your breasts now?" she asked.

"I don't know."

"Mine are bigger than last year," she said.

She pulled open the elastic collar of her dress and showed me a cotton training bra. She tossed her Alice-in-Wonderland blonde hair back over her shoulders.

"Well. Let's see yours."

I untucked my checked shirt from my jeans and lifted it up. "Ooh," she said, "you've got dark nipples." I felt a blush of shame course through me. Her hair was blonde; mine was a tangle of muddy curls. Her nipples were pink; mine were an unseemly dark shade, like eggplant. I knew my face in the dusk was plain and pinched like my mother's.

I got Papa's bridle from its peg. It was an ancient thing with cross reins and a breast harness for barrel racing. I'd polished it many times, a painful process, particularly in the hot summer: so much leather to rub back and front with saddle soap, so many bits of plated silver.

"You be Lady Birkwith," I said. "I'll tie you in the hold."

She rolled her eyes but agreed, lowering herself reluctantly onto the hay-strewn floor of the empty stall. She held out her hands and I laced the reins around her wrists.

"Ouch, that pinches," she said. I unhooked the clip of the harness and wrapped it around her forearms, over her breasts. I watched my dark weasel hands knot the leather around the steel base of the manger. We looked at each other and Serena giggled.

"This is so silly," she said.

"I know." The white leather of her saddle shoe glowed where it stuck out in front of her. I pushed back her skirt on her thigh.

"What are you doing?" she giggled.

"Just something." The sun had sunk beneath the high window. I ran my fingers along the straps of her training bra.

"Oh, Pirate," she laughed. "Don't do that."

"I'll do what I like," I sneered. Then I whispered, "The sweet torture of my hands are touching the bodice of your dress." I pushed up her skirt until her white underwear showed. Then I pushed my finger against the cotton crotch.

"Don't," she said suddenly.

"Why not?"

"I don't like it."

"Too bad."

I pulled back the elastic of her underwear at the leg and looked at her vagina which was bare still, like a child's.

"Untie me," she hissed.

"No."

"You untie me this instant or I'm going to tell Aunt Mary."

I felt like I was falling. "I don't care." I took a piece of hay and dabbed it in a mound of fresh green manure, then I ran it along the white leather of her shoes, over her frilled ankle socks, and up her dress. I smudged it across the pink sateen-covered barrettes and dabbed it on each of her cheeks. She started to cry.

"Be quiet," I said. "They'll hear you." She cried like a child, not caring what noise she made. I shook her a bit, but she started crying harder.

"Stop it."

"You let me go," she wailed.

"Stop it, or I'm going to smack you."

She let out another howl and I slapped her across the face. My palm tingled. She stopped crying abruptly and looked at me.

"Please," I whispered. "Stop crying and I'll let you go."

Her mouth turned down and she drew a long gulp of air, then let out another howl.

"I'm going then," I said. I stood up and walked out of the stall. I closed it behind me and leaned against the door. She kept crying.

"I'm going," I called out to her, and this time I did. I slid the door closed behind me and walked down the road, across the flats to the base of Sauble Mountain. I climbed up the path until I came to my favourite rock, which had retained heat in the dusk like a warm-blooded animal. I sat on it, looking down at the flats, the barn, the house.

Night came. I heard Mother hollering, our collie Freya barking, then Clara's concerned voice. Two black figures approached the barn and went in. Then, a short while later, they came out. Serena's silhouette blended with her mother's. I waited until the moon came up, large and full, until the rock had grown cold and I was shivering. Then I walked back down. The bunch grass looked cool and very clear and the stars overhead shone with a painful brilliance.

My heels ground the dirt as I crossed the turn-around. Then I saw a glint of silver near the horse barn, in the shadow of the ponderosa pine – it was Mother, the bit of Papa's bridle dangling from her hand. I walked across the bright yard and stood near her. She stared at the ground.

"I don't know why I did it," I said.

"Why did you use Papa's bridle?" Her voice quavered in the dark.

My tears were a dark tar I couldn't release. She still made no move to punish me, the bridle hung limp in her hand, and when she looked up I saw she was also close to crying. If I crossed the moonlit dirt she would reach out and enfold me, I would breathe the suede of her jacket. Then a breeze bristled the pine, the moon went behind a cloud. "Mother?" I called because I couldn't see her face. She was against me, I felt her clench my collar.

"You're a bad girl, aren't you?"

"No," I said. "It was Serena –"

"You're a very bad girl." I felt her breath on my face.

She yanked me around to face the stable wall. "Say you're bad," she said, pulling up my shirt. "I'm bad," I cried, as the reins whistled through the air, biting into my back. I clung to the siding as she hit me with a blind relish.

Afterwards, as I lay on my bed in the dark, the door opened. It was Clara; I could tell from the smell of lemony talcum. She was wearing a Chinese-style dressing gown of turquoise and red satin which rustled stiffly as she sat on the side of the bed. I thought at first she was stroking my head, but then I realized she was combing my hair.

"People do things they regret," she said.

I didn't say anything. She worked away at the knots in silence. "Papa hurt your mother once," she said at last. "Perhaps you know that." Mother had never told me this. But when Clara told me, I knew I had always known, that I'd been born with this knowledge, that I'd carried it with me from beyond my earliest memories and dreams.

Mother died of pelvic cancer when I was seventeen. She's buried in the flat expanse of graves near Keremeos. I picked out a slab as marker, nothing else. It says:

> *I've gone to where the darkness ends,*
> *To where the wind blows free,*
> *I've gone away from this small world,*
> *To face my master eternally.*

I don't think she would have liked it, especially the part about the master.

Fourteen floors down, I can hear the thud of cars crossing the steel bridge that draws the four lanes from the QEW into the three lanes of the Gardiner. Beyond is the grey body of the lake, untouchable, serenely polluted. When I close my eyes at last I travel down the freeway, past the frozen neck of the lake, and I look down on the moonlit farm, the whispering corn flats, the old horse barn. Black and white and grey and dun and roan, the horses wait, blowing through their noses. Mother's teeth gleam where she sits on Douna, under the soughing pine. I swing behind, resting my body against her back, and then we begin to canter toward the top of the mountain.

ELIZABETH HAY

Hand Games

It must have had a small, almost invisible beginning, or else I was so intent on believing that nothing was the matter that I missed it. I remember my growing sense of dismay, and my almost constant inner refrain that children are resilient. And I remember one afternoon that came to seem like the beginning, not of the bad time but of my awareness of the bad time.

I was walking down the street ahead of my daughter Annie and her friend Joyce. We paused frequently. Joyce was wearing black patent leather shoes, and every hundred yards she bent down to wipe off the dust. The shoes were tiny and new, and she dusted them off with a white handkerchief. She was very small for four. Annie was the same age but much taller and puppy-like.

We weren't far from home. The streets were lined with old trees and the sidewalk was yellow with leaves. I was carrying a bag of groceries in my right hand. Just before we got to the corner, I felt Joyce's small hand slide into my free hand, leaving the other one for Annie.

The game unfolded. Annie took my encumbered hand. For a while she said nothing, then she whimpered – insisted – that I put the bag in my other hand. I told her not to be silly. Joyce said nothing. She'd said nothing when she ran ahead of Annie to slide her hand into mine, creating this deliberate, wordless, artful triangle.

The two girls were dressed in yellow and pink, and yet they reminded me of dark illustrations in an old storybook. *Dwarf with Dog* would be the caption. I saw my daughter gambolling at the feet of a tiny, dark, compact master. I saw myself in my daughter and my mother in myself – a long and sorry line of tail-wagging.

That morning on the front steps Joyce had kept one hand in her bulging pocket.

Annie asked, "What's in your pocket?"

"Nothing."

"Tell me."

"*Nothing.*"

I lay awake at three in the morning and my daughter's face floated up, the moment when the two girls were coming down the stairs of Annie's school. We'll make hot chocolate, I said to them. Annie turned to Joyce and with a bright smile asked if she wanted hot chocolate. Joyce responded in a low voice. I was ahead of them and didn't catch the words. I caught the tone. I turned and saw my daughter's face widen, a pond into which a stone had been thrown.

We walked home. For a while they played, and then Annie asked for her toy phone. She held out her hand and Joyce walked over with it. A foot away Joyce stopped, put the phone to her own ear, turned her back, and began to talk to Wendy and Peter Pan. Annie lay on the sofa holding a doll to her chest. I saw her face wiped clean, glassy, the outermost reaches of the ripple. And did nothing.

Immobilized by the snake – the touch of the snake – the knowledge that someone can turn against you when you've done nothing wrong; the cavalier nature of friendship; the arbitrary nature of dislike; the twist of rejection; the fall from grace. All of these were present in that small configuration in the dark living room: one child lying on the sofa with averted eyes, the other talking into the toy phone, her back turned.

I did nothing. I didn't know what to do. I was afraid to scold Joyce because she was the daughter of an old friend.

Small hand in mine: soft warm devious hand brushing against mine as though with affection and need. I felt my palm mapped with her ill intentions, implicated in the betrayal of my daughter, pulled into the small child's canny vindictiveness – an intricate, serious, unhappy world. I played along with her even as I saw the game, drawn into the sophisticated world of the smaller child. Impressed by it.

Impressed by the meticulous words she was able to print, by the drawings, complex with colour and minute shapes. Seduced by the seriousness of the child, and intimidated.

Dwarf. Child/adult simultaneously. The interruption of a natural progression. We see a dwarf and are transfixed by the sight of adulthood in the form of a child forever estranged from adulthood, and we look away embarrassed and afraid.

Annie comes home. She comes through the door, hangs on the knob, leans into the door and then into me. She says, "Joyce did everything to hurt my feelings," and her face finally runs with tears.

It wasn't always this way. We moved into this building in September, and for two months their friendship flourished in a form of Eden. The bad time – the first and worst bad time – began in November and went on for two months. Joyce would run to her small rocking chair and hiss, "This chair is my chair, this chair is my chair," low enough so that her mother couldn't hear but loud enough so that Annie heard, so that I heard – the woman who did nothing. She planted her tiny feet and stretched her arms across the hallway so that Annie couldn't pass. She pounced on Annie's mistakes. "That's not a jumping, it's a jumper. That's not a bicycle, it's a tricycle. That's not a skirt, it's a kilt."

At night Annie lay in bed under Joyce's bedroom and listened to the sounds upstairs. She wrapped her handkerchief around her hand and pretended it was broken. She breathed on the window, then drew a heart in the moisture and said, "I'm drawing a heart for Joyce."

Joyce likes to fold towels and pillow cases. I've watched her make the corners meet precisely and smooth the surfaces. She builds neat piles and guards them. After any trip, no matter how short, she goes into her bedroom and touches all the stuffed animals. Her mother has told me this. I suspect she doesn't have names for them. She doesn't pretend they are anything but what they are. But she likes them. When her sisters throw them off the shelf, I've seen her grab the nearest arm and pinch. She gets punished but she doesn't seem to mind this kind of punishment: the sister removed, the door closed, the silence. She puts the animals back on the shelf, always in the same order: soft blue donkey with faded ribbon, rougher older larger bear, white owl, grey rabbit, brown rabbit, cloth rabbit, white lamb, purple hippo – blue, brown, white, grey, brown, pale yellow, white, purple. She arranges colours in her drawings with the same care. When anyone compliments her on her drawings, and they often do, she doesn't acknowledge the compliment. And she never holds up a drawing to say look at this.

Annie puts her hand in mine and feels the hard ridge of plastic, the reduced space for her own hand, the weight of groceries pulling my arm down, my quick step; and there is Joyce, on the other side, with my free hand all to herself.

The softest part of my hand is the palm and the hardest part is the bottom of the fingers. They are the hardest and coldest part. Annie tells me, "My skin is soft and your skin is hard."

She brushes against my leather jacket and looks down at the sidewalk, which is uneven and dusty. People pass by and say of Joyce, "How adorable, is she yours?" "No," I say, "she's a friend."

Annie tries to take Joyce's hand and sometimes Joyce lets her, and sometimes Joyce tightens her hand into a fist, and sometimes she jerks her hand away, and sometimes she pushes Annie away.

We walk up the steps to our building. We rent the first floor, Joyce's family has the second, a family with three boys lives on the third, an old woman on the fourth. Six wide steps lead up to the blue front door. At the top of the steps, Joyce and Annie scramble for the wealth of menus left by all the pizzerias in the neighbourhood. Joyce gets four, Annie gets two. "Inside you'll share them," I say.

In the kitchen Joyce slides into Annie's chair and says, "I'm the guest."

Annie looks at me. I look away and say yes, that's right, Joyce is the guest.

Increasingly, I have been feeling the weight of Joyce's jacket. It is soft, bright pink, a year old. The weather has turned cold. Today I ask Joyce if she would like to wear her coat and she gives a fierce shake of her head. I drape the coat over the back of the stroller in which the baby is sleeping, and we walk across the street to get Annie. The girls go to different schools, and twice a week I pick up Joyce as well as Annie.

In the hallway I button up Annie's coat, adjust her hat, and say to Joyce, "You can wear the coat or you can put it over your arm but you have to carry it."

Joyce is holding one of her drawings, she says she can't carry her coat as well.

"Put the drawing in the stroller then." And I reach for it.

Joyce steps back. Refuses.

"You have to carry your coat, Joyce. Each of us is responsible for her own coat. I'm not going to carry it."

I know the coat could be shoved easily into a corner of the stroller, or draped over the back. But I am irritated because my ploy hasn't worked and because I am using a ploy. Now that the train of events has been set in motion, it will play itself out in full.

I insist. Joyce refuses. I take the coat, which has a hood, and drop the hood over Joyce's head. We set off. I have to buy vegetables. Half-way down the block Joyce is crying, darkly furious and on the verge of a tantrum, that the coat is slipping off her, that she has to hold her picture. Outside the vegetable store, she lets the jacket fall to the sidewalk. A passerby picks it up and hands it to me, and I drop the hood over her head. By this time she is storming – loud piercing cries, choked sobs – that her mother never makes her do this – her mother always puts her coat on the stroller – my mother – sob – my mother . . .

I bend down, by now trembling, and tell her that I don't care what her mother does, nor does her mother do that; if she doesn't carry her coat – I hear myself say – there won't be any hot chocolate.

"I don't want hot chocolate," she screams.

"I don't care what you want, I am not carrying your coat."

I push the stroller on, and with trembling fingers choose from the outdoor display four tomatoes, three green peppers, a bunch of parsley. Joyce stands in full tantrum in the middle of the sidewalk, the jacket on the ground except for one sleeve which she holds in her hand. I push the stroller inside the store, my daughter follows, so does Joyce.

"What's the matter?" someone asks.

"Nothing's the matter," I answer. "She doesn't like her coat."

The cashier smiles sympathetically, but I don't care if the cashier is sympathetic. I pay. The children and the coat follow me back outside. Joyce drags it, but she doesn't leave it behind.

Sickness and holidays intervene, and two weeks pass before I pick up Joyce again. I climb the stairs to her school, pick up her lunchbox and her coat, and we go downstairs together. At the door I give Joyce her coat and bend down to see to my son in the stroller. I say, "Joyce, you can wear your coat zipped up or unzipped. Which is it going to be?"

Joyce stands by the door, coat in hand, looking down. I feel the ground give way as I face this dark child.

I finish with the baby. "Zipped or unzipped?"

"Unzipped," she says, and puts it on.

It is bitterly cold. The coat slides off her shoulders and blows wide in the wind.

"Are you cold?" I ask. She shakes her head. "I can zip it up for you." Shake of the head.

We pick up Annie from her school and walk several blocks. Joyce is shivering and nothing is said. Annie starts to talk about her approaching birthday. She will be five. Joyce has already had her birthday, three weeks back.

Then Joyce speaks. She says to Annie, "I'm not coming to your birthday and I'm not giving you a present."

Annie looks at me – slow motion towards tears – and I bend down and speak to Joyce. I say that she has had her birthday, and now Annie is going to have hers; you can't say mean things about it; apologize. Joyce is also close to tears. She says she is sorry. Then as I stand up she says something else, softly. The look on Annie's face makes me ask sharply, "What did you say, Joyce?"

"My mother says I don't have to come."

I try to remember what it was like to be lost in such obstinacy. Some days I can remember and some days I can't.

My friendship with Joyce's mother has changed. I lie awake at night talking to her, but in person I say nothing. At night I tell her that I can't stand it any more. I ask her what we should do. Old scenes between Joyce and Annie play out in my mind. But I know Norma has plenty of problems and doesn't need more. And I'm afraid that once I start to recount the things that Joyce has done to Annie, our friendship will never be the same. But it isn't the same now. We talk to each other, ignoring our daughters, pretending these things aren't happening, and each of us is glad when the other leaves.

Joyce makes our friendship unsustainable, and yet it continues. I continue to pick up Joyce out of loyalty to Norma, and out of my inability to find phrases for what I feel.

Other children live on the block. Linnea lives across the street. She and Joyce have been going to the same school since they were two. Later Linnea's role in the story will become clear to me. It is always clear to Annie.

Annie continues to say, "Joyce is my *best* friend, right? Joyce is my *best* friend."

At her insistence, I take her by the hand up the flight of stairs to Joyce's apartment. I ask Norma if Joyce would like to play.

Norma turns to her daughter. "Would you like to go down?"

"No." The answer is no.

I smile. "Another time."

I hurry Annie away, not up another flight to find another playmate and teach her about the possibility of other friends, the importance of going on, but downstairs and inside. To be especially kind? No, especially irritated. Angry. At being

reminded of my own childhood and forced to realize it will happen again.

I begin to invent excuses: they're not home; it's suppertime;
they're out of town.

I pretend to phone, dialling with one finger and holding the
receiver down with the other. "They're not home," I say.

After a few days, enough time so that Annie won't seem to be
begging for friendship, I give in and we go upstairs.

The staircase is carpeted and wide. Annie's right hand holds
the wooden railing – cool and hard and smooth – and we walk up
into the smell of cooking from the floors above, and down the
hall to Joyce's door.

"Ring the bell," says Annie.

I reach up and ring it, and I hear Joyce's voice. "Linnea, Mom!
It's Linnea!"

Joyce swings the door open and Norma appears at her side.
Behind them is Joyce's special tea set, pink and new and never
brought out for Annie to play with. I say quickly, "Would Joyce
like to come down to play, or do you have other plans?"

Norma hesitates. Then she says, "Annie can stay and play, I
don't mind."

Annie, already inside, stays.

It wasn't possible – why wasn't it possible? – for Norma to say
that she had invited Linnea to play. It wasn't possible for me to
say what I knew, and that we would come back another time.

An hour later I returned for Annie. Linnea was there, and
Linnea's mother.

Joyce said to Annie, "You can go now."

Norma reproached her. "Now, Joyce."

This had been going on the whole time.

"There are different things you can do," I say to Annie. "When
Joyce is mean you can tell her to stop being mean. You can tell
her you don't like it. You can walk away and climb into a chair
and read a book."

Annie has come down from upstairs. She has stopped crying.
She is on the sofa leaning her head against my shoulder.

A few hours later I tuck her into bed and she says, "Talk to me more about Joyce."

"About what you can do?"

"Yes."

"You can just walk away from her and play on your own."

She doesn't say anything. She is holding my hand. Then she says, "I don't want you to pick up Joyce anymore."

I look out the window. A yellow taxi is parked across the street and I think of some tragedy, nothing specific, just the general idea of something unbearable and how I might react. The disbelief, finding myself in a situation recognizable from literature, saying to myself – this is Shakespearean. A misunderstanding of such proportions, an incident so earthshattering, as to make one's life like a book worth reading. The thought injects a certain distance, and the distance a certain relief.

But five-year-olds aren't Shakespearean. They can't even read.

2

On the last day of January I come home, insert my key in the first door to the apartment – the apartment has two doors at either end of a long hallway – and see the farther door swing shut. I go still. My husband is at work and no one is home.

I open the door, look the length of the apartment, and see no one. I find a neighbour on the third floor and together we look through the apartment. I go outside. I see another neighbour and tell her, and once more we comb the apartment. But there is no one. No explanation.

Later I mention it to a friend.

"You saw the future," he says.

What I saw was a triangle of pink: the triangle formed by the doorway and the closing door, and the colour mysterious because the door was brown and the paint in the kitchen was white.

In the afternoon I heard a child's voice in the hallway and felt dismay. Listened – no. Listened – yes. Linnea. Linnea was going upstairs to play with Joyce. I felt such pity, such mortified sadness for my daughter who hadn't been invited. I was transfixed by the pattern repeating itself from childhood. In having a daughter I had rubbed my own childhood into view, and was still rubbing, bent over that worn engraving and rubbing it into view – a picture that emerged through touch rather than sight, and in that way of childhood: knees on the floor, busy fingers, paper and pencil.

I wrote to my mother. In passing I mentioned Joyce. You remember, the aloof and solitary child with a mean streak. I said I had almost come to hate her. That's all.

But as I wrote, my own relationship with my mother – that awkward unhappy thing – came back to mind. My own refusal to please. How else could it be described? I used to sit on the verandah steps and deliberately withdraw. I knew that I had a choice. I could laugh when I was teased and win my parents' approval and my mother's gratitude, or I could sulk and fume. I chose to sulk, though that isn't the best word to describe the combination of fury and helplessness and pleasure which I chose to inhabit because it satisfied me more than cheerfulness, especially cheerfulness as practised by my mother – an unfailing attitude, a permanent posture. With my mother, pleasing and pleasure were the same.

My mother wrote back. I'm sorry, she said. I caught her tone, the shake of the head, the unspoken "it's a shame." An end-of-the-world tone, useless, completely useless to me.

Where does it come from, this end-of-the-world thinking? The belief that one bad thing cancels out everything else? It must be the panic of childhood retained. So that in the face of one criticism everything else, everything positive, the continuous ground we stand upon, falls away. A slight by Joyce of Annie, a criticism of my husband by a colleague, and the world drops away.

Why do some people retain the sense of a continuous world around them, and others not?

I ask Joyce to wait in her cubby, and I go into the teacher's office, which is off to one side. I say, "I need some advice."

The teacher asks me if I have talked with Norma. I shake my head. "She's a dear friend, I'm picking up Joyce to help her out." I shake my head again.

"You may have to," says the teacher, "but there are two other things you can do. You can say to them, 'You don't have to like each other all the time, you don't have to play with each other all the time, but you do have to be nice to each other.' And you can separate them. Put one of them to play by herself in one room, and the other in another room."

The teacher's voice is very loud. I move to close the door tightly, and the teacher continues to talk just as loudly. Doesn't she care if Joyce hears? Does she want her to know she's being talked about? Does she think that will help? She says that little girls, especially, are like this.

We finish talking and I leave her office. Joyce is still sitting in her cubby, her face sombre and unreadable. We go down the stairs and across the street to Annie's school. Every few feet of our progress, I congratulate myself that things are going smoothly, that I am calm, that I haven't given Joyce any rope to hang me with.

The teacher said, "Your daughter needs your protection. You must interfere."

I say to both children, "We have a new rule. You don't have to play together, but you have to be nice to each other." And I set up two spots, the rocking chair where Joyce can go to sit by herself, the sofa for Annie.

When they quarrel I try something I read in a book. I ask each of them to tell me what's the matter. Annie tells me. Joyce won't. I guess what's the matter with Joyce and she nods. Then I tell them to go and sit on my bed. "Close the door, talk it out for five minutes, come back with a solution."

I am amazed when they come back smiling and tell me what they have decided.

I watch them sometimes through the glass door, conferring on the bed. They sit side by side, as though on a park bench, and sometimes they come back after a few minutes and sometimes they remain. But the problem, the quarrel, goes away.

In a few weeks they are closer friends than they have ever been.

They play house, castle, boat, pirate ship, camping. They pull around the furniture in the living room, drape it with old pieces of material, add the little table and chairs from Annie's bedroom; they erect walls with square pieces of old foam and fashion a rooftop from a long flat cushion. The little areas they make are small and beautiful, and often so carefully arranged with pieces of old black lace and rose-covered fabric that they look Japanese. The two of them in combination, not alone, make these places and play quietly for hours.

These little tents of friendship – creative and flimsy, improvised from big and little, different each time – have enough space for just the two of them; they sit under the shelter of an old shawl roof and pour themselves pretend tea.

I watch the two girls become friends again, unable to put my finger on how it happens and aware that everything might crumble again.

It does. Once again Joyce turns against Annie.

It happens one afternoon after two hours of happy playing. Joyce fights with one of her sisters and is sent to her room. But it is Annie she insults. From her bed she yells, "Annie Pinhead." And again. "Annie Pinhead."

Annie hears Joyce. She smiles and walks towards me. A tentative half-smile that doesn't last.

Norma goes into Joyce's room, pulls her out into the kitchen and tells her to apologize. She won't. Her mother shakes her. She still won't.

"You'll apologize tomorrow then," and pushes her back towards her room.

On the outs. It's almost a crack down the side of your body, a shade you occupy while others sit in the sun. A dark brassiness, metallic, exposed, abandoned to the weather. And yet you choose it and not just because it's familiar. You formulate plans – not plans of action, plans of emotion.

The streetlight comes on and I imagine that Joyce raises her gaze. She looks out the window at Linnea's house and pictures a special tea party, just the two of them, with ice cream and real tea and sugar cubes.

Someone she recognizes – one of the mothers – goes into Linnea's house. Linnea has been playing with Matthew, and now he's coming out with his mother. Tall skinny Matthew has been playing with tall skinny Linnea.

Her mother comes into the room. She is urgent, emphatic, determined, worried. "You can't treat your friends this way," she says, "or you won't have any friends."

But Joyce knows this isn't so. She knows that Annie will always come running.

3

My mother comes to visit. One evening she helps Annie with her homework. I lie on the sofa and listen to her soft relentless voice. "What does this say? Sound it out. What sound does this letter make? What letter is it? What sound does it make?"

The soft patience which at any moment will turn sharp. And here it is. "How did you get *that*?"

Annie begins to chew on her hand. She puts the side of her thumb into her mouth, then the side of her hand, making small wet teeth marks. Her grandmother says, "Don't," and pushes her hand out of her mouth. "It will get sore."

I look at the furniture while this is going on. The light from the standing lamp falls through the mesh on the big armchair and makes a pattern on the soft velvet seat. I don't interfere any more than I interfere with Joyce. I listen, and relive my mother's voice directed similarly at me. The quiz, where the adult knows the answer and you don't. Where the adult pretends she is helping when, in fact, she is testing.

I hear my voice (it is my mother's voice) quizzing my daughter and my mother quizzing me – the pattern has splayed wider – and I feel pain on my child's behalf, and on my own behalf, and on my mother's behalf, since although she appears to be the source of this unreasonable and unnecessary unhappiness, how can she be? Someone came before her too.

In the morning I make coffee, and try to say something that my husband won't dismiss as extreme. I don't say that I feel as if I'm in the presence of evil. I don't say that Joyce is full of raw newborn malice. I say that Annie doesn't seem to have as much stamina as her two-year-old brother. My husband looks at me.

"Don't you remember?" he asks. "When Annie was two she had just as much stamina." And he describes the way she would get up at five in the morning and run around the kitchen with arms held high.

It comes back to me then, a vision of happy exuberance. I feel the size and weight of that plump little body, remember the expressions on her face, and the irrepressible personality. Bright, tough, funny, tender. Now, three years later, here she is. Taller, skinnier, and burdened, somehow, with temperament.

"Her life is much harder and more complicated now," he says. "She's much more aware of the world out there, and she has friendships to deal with."

A phrase goes through my mind. The stress of friendship. How early that kicks in.

When I finally react, I overreact. Perhaps it's because so many peaceful months have gone by. Perhaps that's why I can't bear the next falling out. It's summer. School has ended. The two girls haven't seen each other for two weeks because my daughter has chosen a day camp that offers swimming, and Joyce doesn't want to swim. Annie hasn't asked to see Joyce until now. She goes upstairs to play, and after twenty minutes comes back. "Joyce told me to leave," she says. And the tears begin.

For the next two weeks Joyce is deliberately cold and punitive. Annie is pensive, but how unhappy it's hard for me to say. I am fierce. I tell Annie that Joyce is not welcome in our home. I say, "Her sort of behaviour isn't allowed."

My husband objects. "Are you sure it's wise?"

But I am strident, determined. Annie has to learn to steel herself. She has to learn what I was never taught. She has to learn not to be taken for granted.

Annie wants to know if we are never going to invite Joyce again.

"Not until she invites you," I say. "Let her take the first step. I won't allow you," I say, "to invite her."

Several times over the next week Annie broaches the subject. We will be on the street and she will say, "We're never going to invite Joyce?" And then she will say that Joyce is her oldest friend and she is Joyce's oldest friend. "We knew each other since we were babies. We've been friends since we were one year old, two years old, three years old, four years old, five years old. Joyce and Linnea are just friends since they started going to school." She is building a faith as she skips along beside me.

We pass a fruit store and she is framed by fresh tomatoes, oranges, the first strawberries. I look down at her and see her trying to soften and reassure me. My attempt to harden her makes her even softer. She is handling me the way she handles Joyce.

A few days later Joyce initiates a visit and it goes completely smoothly, as does almost every visit after that.

When I think back on the whole period, I know that most of the time – eighty percent of the time – the two girls were fast friends. A pattern of intimacy controlled and periodically broken by Joyce. I don't know whether they adjusted to each other or whether Annie adjusted – gave way – to Joyce. Whatever happened was invisible and miraculous and temporary. They would be down by the river, fishing out leaves, nuzzling a lunch of orange slices on a blanket – grazing, I thought, as I heard their wet little mouths working – and I would be impressed by their diplomacy and affection, by the simplicity and sophistication of their forgiveness. I would feel relieved and wary. Months would go by without a break, months when the friendship was the most stable part of their lives and whatever troubles they had they resolved themselves. And then something would happen.

What happened, I realize, was always the same. Joyce would pull away and Annie would wait for her to come back.

"I wait for the other day," she told me.

"For another day?"

"Yes. She says she's never going to be my friend, and the next day she's my friend again."

One child knew all about power and the other learned all about patience.

I should have expected the final trouble, but it took me by surprise. A cool summer preceded this last episode. One morning Norma came down with a bag of clothes. All week she'd been packing and setting aside warm things as unnecessary. Joyce was on her heels. She insisted on keeping several things and uncharacteristically her mother gave in. Suddenly there was an area of yielding that hadn't been there before, an eagerness to compensate for all the upheaval. They were moving south.

I watched Joyce enter this new emotional territory. Her grandmother catered to her more than ever, her parents softened their criticism, friends made arrangements to see her for the last time; they brought gifts, they cried. It seemed to me she enjoyed the narrowing of focus, the paring away of possessions, the simplifying of life even as it became more complicated. This was a process she was adept at, riding a storm in a narrow and purposeful boat.

That summer my daughter learned several hand games. She played them fast and with tremendous merriment. There would be the slapping of palm against palm – knee – shoulder – palm in patterns that were intricate and ingenious and rewarding. Annie's face was brown and attentive and relaxed.

Joyce was good at not playing; at making you feel foolish for wanting to play.

This would be their final summer together.

Two days before they moved away, Norma and I talked about our daughters. It happened the morning after the going-away party, after Annie's confused sorrow and my relief that there would be no more of this. I walked upstairs and knocked on Norma's door.

Norma was packing. She listened and said, "I'm so sorry. I didn't know."

"It's not all bad," I said. "Annie has to learn how to protect herself. She has to learn not to wear her heart on her sleeve."

"But that's the wonder of her," said Norma, and she leaned against the doorway, slender and tired and worried.

The night before, Annie and I left the going-away party early to sit on the lower bunk in her room. It was dark outside. The window was open and the sounds of the party drifted down. It had been raining all day.

Annie listened to my voice – low and hesitant – say that Joyce was about to move and would miss her very much.

She didn't believe me. She said, "She won't even remember me because I didn't sign the book." And she cried quietly.

She meant the guest book. It was on a small table beside the large table of food, and friends had been writing their names, addresses, sentimental farewells. For most of the party Joyce wouldn't speak to Annie. She wouldn't acknowledge her presence. Linnea was there and several of Joyce's cousins. Even after Linnea left, even after the cousins went home, Joyce wouldn't speak to Annie or look at her.

"I know Joyce doesn't like me – she's sick of me – she didn't play with me all night – she won't even remember me because I didn't sign the book."

"You can sign the book tomorrow."

"She didn't even talk to me."

"You know what Joyce is like. You know how nasty she can be sometimes."

"I know she can be nasty, but I don't know *when*."

I sat on the edge of the bunk and didn't know what to do. Should we take Joyce's cue and not bother to say goodbye? Should we wait until moving day and expect her to say goodbye then? Should we let her define the friendship?

This last thought was the one that cut through my anger, and I heard myself suggest that Annie make a going-away card for Joyce.

"Would you like to?"

Annie said she would. The suggestion seemed to relieve her. She put her head on the pillow and fell asleep.

The next morning I went upstairs. My heart felt loose inside me and I said too much too apologetically. It shouldn't be so hard to be straightforward.

Around us was the chaos of the move. Norma was wearing a dress she had intended to give away, but under the stress of the move she had lost so much weight that it finally fit. It looked lovely on her and I said so.

"What should we do?" I asked.

"What if I made a time for them to play together by themselves? Later this afternoon? I'll extend an invitation."

In the afternoon the sisters came down to invite Annie and

her brother to watch a movie. They came down first, and then they came down again with Joyce because they wanted to start the movie right away; they wanted Annie and her brother to hurry up.

"Hi, Joyce," Annie said with a small and hopeful smile.

Joyce didn't reply. She stood out in the hallway and looked away.

Annie waited a moment and then repeated, "Hi, Joyce."

Joyce, without looking at her, said hi.

Annie looked at me then with the same hopeful smile, but wider, even more hopeful, and full of relief. She was reassuring me that everything was all right.

The next day Joyce's family moved away. In the hour before their departure Joyce and Annie played. Quietly, at first, and on the sofa. They sat side by side. Then they went outside onto the street where the moving van was being filled. They hung on the fence, they ran and scampered and laughed.

Just before they left Norma gave me a card that Joyce had made for Annie but "forgotten" to give to her. Joyce didn't forget to show Annie Linnea's gift of writing paper. This she made a special trip upstairs to get; this she displayed, full of smiles; this she hugged to her chest.

Now I look up from grating a cabbage and see Norma through the window – same hair, same sweater. I start, and the woman catches sight of me and smiles. It's the sweater. A heavy dark brown and white sweater that Norma used to wear in the fall. And the loose thick hair.

I see Joyce too, but not in the same way, or in any way that I could have predicted. I see her in Annie.

A new family has moved in upstairs. One of the children is Annie's age and they are in the same class. In the morning the new girl, Marcela, runs up to Annie and Annie turns away.

Norma at the window, and Joyce in Annie – the absence of a smile, and something more than shyness.

I think of my mother, a woman with no protective shell. She

is porous to everyone she meets and this is difficult for them as well as for her. They feel invaded by an innocent country, and she feels taken aback to learn that she isn't welcome. There is no end to her when she is with other people, no solitude. She wants, like a child, to be included and at the centre of everything. And yet this doesn't occur out of egotism, at least not of the usual kind, but out of friendliness; the egotism of the shy perhaps. Not that she is shy, but shyness shaped her, and the desire to be liked.

I have seen my mother treated the way Joyce treated Annie. Seen her greet someone with great friendliness, someone dark and shy and reserved and cruel, and seen that person not respond. Seen my mother repeat her cheery greeting more cheerily: "I said hello." And seen the response: "I know."

A cool and rude young man irked by her overeagerness. It wasn't just his coolness, his rudeness; it was her effort, her inability to be easy about friendship, her obvious need to have people like her. The new girl upstairs has this quality, this willingness to be hurt.

Joyce so small, so concentrated, with those hunting headlights in her eyes, and the highway so wide and dark. Her cruelty took the form of savage silences, calculated and cool and sophisticated. Women treat men this way – men they want to punish, men they want to keep.

"Such a mean streak," Norma said once.

And I softened it, reassured her. We all have mean streaks, she's not a mean child.

I lied. I hoped. I reassured. I misunderstood. I thought she was a child who didn't suffer fools gladly, a child driven by a principled refusal to please. In her cubby at school she never looked up. Other children raced around and shouted when their mothers and babysitters arrived. Joyce didn't. She wouldn't give me, wouldn't give her mother, the satisfaction of getting what we wanted. She saw the expectation in our faces, however muted, felt it in the stance of our bodies as we waited for her to stand up.

One morning I realized my mistake. I saw her in the schoolground during recess. Her teacher was carrying her on her hip while the other children ran around, and Joyce was playing up to her shamelessly. I had never seen her so happy.

They drove away finally. They moved. And just before moving Joyce took pains to remind Annie who was boss. Don't ever think you don't need me, and don't ever think I need you.

Annie looks for mail every day. She pulls a chair into the hall and stands on it to reach the mailbox. When Joyce's postcard arrives – after days of waiting – Annie sticks it up on the refrigerator door. The postcard says how much Joyce misses her. This is what Annie wanted to hear, all she wanted to hear.

Annie writes a postcard to Joyce. "All I am thinking about is you," she writes. And she says to me, "That's not all I'm thinking about, but that's okay."

A month later she draws a picture of our apartment – the long sofa, the window, the big round overhead light. She writes *shshshsh* across the bottom of the page because, she says, the people upstairs are saying *shhhh*, and the cars outside say *shhhh* when it rains.

I suggest that she send the picture to Joyce but she doesn't want to.

"Would you like to write her a letter?"

No, she doesn't want to do that either. "I wrote to her already."

Joyce in Annie: a more determined child, no less easily hurt but eager to be someone. She sits at the table with her new friends and they compete over who has the most cousins, who has travelled farthest, who has plans to travel soon, and her face runs with feeling. She shows everyone Joyce's postcard, even as a party we attend brings back memories of the going-away party and sparks the comment: "Joyce did that to me." We're standing beside a table of food, and children are chasing each other through the rooms. "Joyce did that to me," she says. And then, "She was thinking she'd never see Linnea again."

"But why would that make her treat you badly?"

She doesn't answer, and later I ask again. "What made Joyce behave that way?"

"We talked about that already," and her face is flushed – embarrassed – private.

How different we are. Why has it taken me so long to realize? She has never believed that Joyce was mean for the sake of being mean. She has always seen the whole thing as an affair of the heart. She was to Joyce as Joyce was to Linnea.

I dream about my daughter. I have taken her to school, into a room crowded with children, and she won't stay. She follows me into the hallway where I scold her endlessly, all the while aware of what others are thinking. They are thinking no wonder the child is so unhappy.

I see everything in stark terms – a child's capacity for evil, my incapacity to protect my child. I see a fatal flaw, something inherited that my mother and I have never been able to shake – a line of rejection passing down. But Annie (who has the clearest eyes, a man said, that he had ever seen) sees, instead, the nature of love.

ELISE LEVINE

Boy

I saw an ocelot, bag of bones with lime-jello eyes. A nest of mud snakes, glazed in the heat like ham. The peccary is indigenous to North and South America. It has sharp tusks, small erect ears, and a short tail. The Virginia opossum is variable, but prefers woodlands. The young attach firmly to a teat and remain for 55 to 70 days.

Did you know each toe of an even-toed ungulate ends in a hoof?

An example is an old world swine.

Texas sliders: most of central Texas and Pecos River. Suwannee cooters: a turtle of the clear spring runs; also occurs in the turtle-grass flats off mouths of streams.

Mudpuppies waving crimson gills. Skin not toxic like many other amphibians.

A bowl of meat dipped in raw egg, smell rising like a man's throat.

Hold your nose, Jamie, my mother said.

A woman squealed.

At the gorilla enclosure two boys tossed sticks. My mother watched from a bench above the dirt path. Smart, she said loudly. The biggest boy screwed up his face at the male gorilla, who mimicked him, then spat green stuff into a black palm and showed it to the crowd. I observed closely the ears and snout, as if cutting a picture from a *National Geographic* my aunt used to send from Florida, curls of paper like toenail clippings on the floor. Sometimes I glued pebbles shaped like molars, tufts of hair from the neighbour's dog to the scrapbook page.

The boys huddled close to the plexiglass. Judging by height, I bumped the youngest. His face folded. Adam, do a payback, the older one said. Trash him. My mother said, Jamie. She sipped her soda, every now and then holding the cup to her wide sweating face, white as the peeled potatoes she cut and French fried six days a week in the back of our truck in Picton. With her free hand she lifted her long thick hair, tangling wet off the back of her muscled neck, and shook it. The boys shuffled off, turning every half-minute or so to look at me. I eased toward them through the Sunday crowd, endless baby strollers, cotton candy, my strawberry Yoo-Hoo drink – from my decreasing Florida supply – warm from the sun.

Adam, whispered the bigger boy. He shook a box of Chiclets. A–dam.

II.

A hundred garter snakes. A hundred-hundred milk snakes.

This was in Fort White.

The first one I saw – rubbery, dry – was wrapped around a leg of the table off which we ate. The second, third, and fourth to seventh scraped furiously under the door to the small storage space off the trailer bathroom, where I'd left them, popping against the sides of a green garbage bag. I'd collected them at lunch time for my science project, two days overdue.

I opened the storage space door. The bag was broken. Snakes flailed the air.

Honestly, my mother said. She stood in the doorway above me, half blocking the light. She came one step down the stairs. Snakes clefted away from her feet. Holy jumpin. Her eyes shone in the semi-dark. She put her hands on her broad hips.

Let's get these out. Pronto.

She turned and stepped back into the hall. Snakes flipped after her up the last step.

Outside the trailer the tall grass lolled. She knelt beside me, right knee creased with scars from an operation. Her square hands, also scarred, leaked grease from the truck's deep fryers onto a brown paper bag which she opened carefully. Seven snakes wrinkled across the narrow drive.

She said, So much for homework.

At school I was average and slipping, dull as rain, what I could figure of meridians, the square of the hypotenuse filling me like an old tin can. At night I slept rust: sea salt, inland springs, Crystal River, the manatees. Spanish moss. Sky red as blood-shame in my ears when Jan-Elizabeth kissed me Wednesday morning at recess, and her girlfriends laughed loud as cicadas.

This was in Madison.

In Perry I play burnball every day after supper, making do with Mike Hires, a retard from Special Ed. class. Slap-slap down the road, smoking ball against glove faster-fast through the long twilight, everything flattened to two boys one creature purely boy, and a sound like spitting.

There are days and days of this.

And fire when I torched the fort with kerosene stolen from the neighbour's shed. Inside the plywood walls one of the boys said, Steve and Jerry. Another one said, No, Ken. I swear it was Ken.

They were older than me. The fort was their meeting place, and I followed them there several times a week for a month until they saw me slipping after them among the trees.

War. My face had ached for days. Now, crawling belly down beneath the skewed hole they called a window, splashing the walls from a tin can, I stopped to wipe sweat from my eyes, crying oil.

Maybe Steve and Ken.

No way. Was not.

More fuel. A dribble leaked from my nose. Then smoke and

flame, a million boy-voices lifting to oaks' old arms high above my escape route.

I made myself scarce for weeks.

Gradually I began to come around again, four o'clock on the outskirts of school, fast squeezes of gravel aching from my bike's tires, girls whose names I never learned twisting in fear when I lunged for their breasts.

If you live near a spring or swamp, you too can collect specimens. Look for mole skinks (Family Scincidae) in areas of sandy well-drained soil. The positions of the longitudinal stripes are important. Count downward from the midline of the back. As in: "stripe on 5th row."

Rule out whiptail lizards by checking back and belly scales.

Hellbenders thick as cushions in specimen jars, tasselled gills waving red.

Palmetto bugs larger by night when I thought I'd turned the light on in the kitchenette and squashed one, then woke suddenly, wet in the bed.

The terrible scent of almonds.

Boy. Pecker like a roach, my mother said.

That was in Branford.

One fall afternoon I heard the truck pull into the drive earlier than usual, the bump and bang of pails of grease she'd change only once a week. What do *they* know, she'd say of her customers, mostly people just passing through who she'd never see again. Let them complain.

I knew she hated being questioned. I'm fit, she'd say after the few parent-teacher interviews she attended at my schools. After the fort burned she'd said, Just let them try.

I hadn't been to this new school once this fall, but I didn't think she knew. When she opened the front door and stepped inside I had an excuse ready. But she didn't seem to notice me as I leaned against the kitchenette counter. She put her bag on the sofa and lifted her left hand to the side of her face, cradling it. She stumped slowly around the room, picking up objects – an old perfume bottle her last boyfriend scrounged diving on the bottom of the river, a giant pinecone her sister bought years ago at a giftshop in California – with her right hand as if weighing all that was past and would never come back, figuring what she could add in or take out according to whatever sense she could make of things to come.

Finally she said, And that's the name of that tune. She put down a white plaster angel she'd been considering.

Jamie.

She came over and took my arms, held them out to her. Then she pinned me, quickly, to the stove, its chipped enamel like tooth marks.

You little bastard.

She let my arms drop. You fucked up, she said. We're out of here. We're goners.

We spent that night at my aunt's in Lake City. Her house was unfamiliar to me, slipcovers on the sofa and soft chairs, and my own room to sleep in.

My aunt had never married – unlike my mother, who'd left my father when I was two, divorced him when I was five – and lived alone in a small bungalow bought with her portion of their mother's inheritance. The *larger* portion, my mother called it: my aunt had looked after the old woman in sickness, who never forgave my mother for leaving. For years the two sisters hardly spoke. My aunt was nuttier than a fruitcake, my mother said – her younger sister periodically checking into a private clinic in Tampa – just like their mother. And as loaded. She was younger than my mother, though they looked alike, my aunt being slightly softer, puffed up and melting where her makeup ran.

I woke the next morning to my aunt opening the bedroom door. Rise and shine.

It was late, ten o'clock at least. I said, Where is she?

Come on, lazy bones, let's get cracking.

She walked all the way into the room. I pulled up the covers. Where did she go?

She snapped back the navy blue curtains and opened the screen window.

Your mother, she said. *Your* mother.

At Wal-Mart my aunt buys extra packages of t.p.

In case we run out.

She laughs giddily, winks, then rolls the cart to the ladies' undergarment aisle, her ankles spongy beneath green pants.

Orange blouse.

We go to the Waffle House for lunch, homefries scattered smothered covered. Chunked? the waitress says. *Not* chunked. My aunt says, Are you sure? and the waitress winks.

I am sure.

The drive home on roads shiny as sheet metal, leftover steak leaking through the doggy-bag onto my lap. A sudden rainstorm bends branches over the road. Just as suddenly, the storm's over.

Well hello sunshine.

A white chair.

Jamie, do you like peas?

That night there was a map of the universe on the ceiling of the room I was now supposed to call mine, star light star bright first star I see tonight bright as the Happy Face nite-lite my aunt bought, oblivious to my age. My mother was still gone. Cassiopeia. Polaris. My aunt's light went out down the hall. The house smelled of freshener and fish cakes.

I got out of bed and flicked on my light. After a moment I turned it off and got back into bed. Ursanus, arcturus, small points of yellowish green, sparked above my head and somewhere outside, firestorms, the collapse of suns and cold distance seeping across the fields of night. The Great Horse Nebula on a hot tear through the fissure cracks and bedding planes of the covering sky. The Happy Face grinning like mad.

Ursanus-arcturus, bright and early, rise and shine. My aunt took the wet bedsheets from my hands.

Uh oh, Geronimo.

Bitch.

My aunt turned to me and said, Go upstairs. This was my fourth day alone in the house with her. I had just finished my third Pop Tart, and now my mother stood on the front steps to the house, impressively kicking the door.

Ellen, please, my aunt said.

My mother thumped the door with her fists. Joy. Give him back, Joy.

My aunt began to cry, slowly shrugging her shoulders. She leaned against the wall and held her stomach as if in her softness something hard and precious might slip to the floor and shatter.

Ellen, don't make me. He's mine. Not yours.

That night my mother and I rode in the truck past Luraville, the road sourly rolling as I knew she'd rolled from Texas once, to Florida's gulf side, slicks moving in like sadness from Corpus Christi, the Padre Islands of her childhood. It was a clear night, and the town lights skipped like stones in the truck's rearview mirror. She turned onto the dirt road to Telford Spring.

She fucked us. I tried to fix things but she fucked us over.

I didn't say anything. The truck bumped along until we reached the clearing. She stopped and said, Here we are.

Thin clouds coiled in the sky. Something hissed at the night then was silent. Through the windshield the water seemed slippery as vinyl. At first only the occasional splish-splash or a low soft guttering heard through the open window gave depth to the tannic river. Neither of us said a word, as if we were waiting for something too important to miss and we wanted to be ready for it.

I could tell from her sharp breathing that she was still fuming. I twisted my back to the door on my side and stretched out anyway, feet in her lap. She snagged my ankles in her hands, and held on tight. The night wore on, the stars above and below the billion wink-sinkings of patio lights. Gradually I forgot right side up and upside down. Fog slid in. I slept.

The next morning we were almost to Valdosta when, as if she still clutched my ankles, I leaned out the truck window, sick onto the I-75 shoulder.

Count the wrinklies, she said each time we passed an RV of old people heading south from Canada. Her half-brother lived there.

We passed our fifth Airstream. How many was that? she said. Sixteen? I think that was sixteen.

~

My small thoughts slipped like pennies all the way to the Ontario border, to Scarborough, to Picton – like the allowances my aunt sent, whatever small change my mother passed on to me and I spent on black balls, the layers sucked past orange, robins' egg blue to grey the colour of Lake Ontario boiling from the Bay of Quinte to Point Traverse where rum-runners once ran and the wet bones of old sailing ships – the *Annie Falconer*, the *Olive Branch*, *City of Sheboygan* – lie in cold silt off False Duck and Amherst Island. Where the money from my aunt stopped coming as winter steam lifted in sheets off the lake warmer than 40-below air.

When the snow turned to rain then to fever and fog I heard a voice tumbling like rags inside a washer saying, Catch me if you can, dissolving in acid, stretched to a shape I couldn't recognize, hung to dry on the crackle-breath of jaws.

Anhinga, snake-bird.

Old copies of *Gator USA*, hoarded for centuries. My mother who runs the chip wagon. She is old and I must do my best to love her, greasy, a mottled anger cooking her bones – in a cold cold land and I do not belong.

My mother's touch soft as the Velveeta I began to crave in spring. A sure sign, she said, I was getting better.

In summer, leopard toads sundering the lighthouse road as I walked, shush-shushing into the long grass, amphibian hearts turning blue in their cold chests.

A hundred-hundred hundred snakes. And I a follower of science.

III.
CROCODILIANS. American Alligator (*Alligator mississippiensis*). Black with yellowish lines. Head smooth in front of eyes.
   Curved bony ridge —>
   4th tooth —>
   You may observe eyes, snouts protruding from water surface of holes along waterways of the south.
   All sizes bask.

My mother fanned herself with a zoo guide. Her empty soda container sat at her feet. She smiled at a young woman in a yellow sunsuit who bent over a small girl and roughly tucked her shirt into her pants. In the exposed part of the woman's breasts tiny blue veins jumped like electrical currents. Before straightening she jerked the girl's pants up. The child rose two inches off the ground.
   I pulled a peanut from my pocket, shucked it one-handed and flicked the shell. It bounced at Adam's feet. My mother wasn't looking. Adam, I called softly. His friend's Chiclets whispered in their box.
   Quit following that boy around – if he jumped off a bridge you'd go too.

Adam, eyes open wide. Pale colouration, short red hair. Approx. four feet, two inches.
   I took a swig of my drink.

The spectacled caiman is small and has a bony ridge between the eyes. Problems of identification occur only in Florida. In the American alligator the snout is broad and rounded in front.

A woman sat next to my mother on the bench. Boys, the woman

said. My mother said, I know what you mean. You can say that
again. She clicked open her purse. She said, Jamie.

I put my Yoo-Hoo on the concrete ledge above the enclosure.
CAUTION. DO NOT LEAN. Nothing in the pool below me moved.
The surface was green, thick as brine from a pickle jar.

The fourth tooth, while enlarged, fits into a pit in the upper
jaw and is not exposed at the side when jaws are closed, as in the
American crocodile.

More soda, my mother called. She pulled a five from her purse.

∼

Voice. Adult Male: throaty, bellowing roar. Adult Female: grunts
like a pig when calling to her young, which she may protect
from predators. Young: high-pitched, moaning grunt – like saying *umph-umph-umph*.

I leaned over the railing, looking in. A musky unpleasant
odour.

Alligators of all sizes hiss.

Adam watched as his friend edged closer to the railing beside
me. Chickenshit. Buck-buck-buck buck. The Dickey Dee wagon
was coming through. When I looked again not even my mother
was there.

IV.
I'm freckled. Jeans rolled up, my high tops on. It's 1993. BOY
EATEN BY GATOR. Another headline might read, BOY KILLED AT
ZOO. But I'm down here, I'm down here still. (Turn the page. See?)
Keeper pokes at me and the crowd thrills to my sluggish moves.
At night his pole glows verdigris, the lights of my pool like stars
dragged down from the sky to where they hiss and gurgle.

Here's another.

A boy peers over the low railing. Cowlick. Peanut fists. Red-
stained mouth, Tahiti Treat. He leans closer. There's a moment
when the crowd looks away.

Yoo-hoo, I call.

MICHELLE ALFANO

Opera

n. *A form of drama in which music is a dominant factor, made up of arias, recitatives, choruses, etc. . . . with orchestral accompaniment, scenery, acting, and sometimes dance.*

I have always known opera to have two meanings in our home, one in its traditional sense and the other meaning was used in the following fashion, as in *"Che é 'sta opera?"* Translation: "What is this drama/noise/chaos?" This was yelled at us by our parents or aunts and uncles whenever we were being particularly loud and disruptive. Which was often.

made up of arias

My mother's favourite opera was *La Traviata*. She would put on the 1958 live recording on the old stereo of Maria Callas singing in Lisbon when she did housework after a shift in the factory. She worked in the cotton mill and rushed home just after dawn to wake and feed me. My crib was in the small bedroom next to the back yard. When I stood on tiptoe I could see the tomato plants from my window and old Mr. Mathews sometimes sleeping on the grass of his back yard next door in the afternoon. My parents' bedroom was on the other side of the house. Sometimes I lay on the bed between my mother and father after she got home and before my father went to work for the city, fixing roads.

My earliest memory is that of my mother dusting and singing to me between arias of *La Traviata*. Pink feathers tickled photographs of our family and large cubes of zirconium on brass disguised as knick knacks. Here is my mother in a shiny black bun and stiletto heels with blood-red lipstick and a beautiful beaded cocktail dress. Here is my father, still lean and handsome then, in a dark suit and thin tie, his arm over my mother's shoulder.

"Do you hear that cough!" she asked as she spoon-fed me some mashed banana after she put on the record. "That means she's going to die. Always listen for the cough, Lilla, that's always a sure sign that they'll be dead in act three." Personally I preferred the "Drinking Song" in act one or the gypsy dancing at the end of act two, something fun and lively. Better than that tired old Violetta and her cough dying of some unknown disease at the end of act three. When she finally took me to see the opera I told Mama I couldn't understand how a 250-pound woman could die of consumption but she just told me to keep quiet.

"I love this part," she said when she put on the record for the first time. In act one after Violetta's soirée in her salon, Alfredo begs to see her once again. She finally agrees after much flirtation. He asks when he can see her, and as he says this, Mama took a plastic rose from a vase on the TV and handed it to me and said, *Take this flower. You shall bring it back when it has withered.* Violetta and her white camelias. Alfredo is thrilled because that means he may return tomorrow. I clapped my hands, my small mouth full of banana, awaiting the next aria.

We lived on Paradise, not Upper Paradise on the mountain, just Paradise. Hamilton "mountain" is actually a hill and has streets which extend upwards from the downtown core. They run roughly the same direction. Generally the houses on "Upper" were newer, nicer, bigger. Ours was a three-storey brick house built before the war and we lived behind a giant billboard. This is a picture of me on my tricycle in front of the billboard. That's my brother Joey standing on the back. When I was small I used to think we owned the billboard because it was on our property. Kids on the streets thought we did too, they said we were rich dagos. I asked Mama if we were and she smacked me and said,

"Don't you dare walk around saying we're rich!" I don't think she was sure what dago meant but she understood rich.

I can still hear her singing to me in my high chair in the kitchen on Paradise Street, especially the "*Croce e Delizia*" aria. Sometimes the roles were reversed and I was her Violetta, she was my Alfredo. She held her duster like a sword. She leaned into my face passionately, her cotton housecoat bunched up in little seams around her heart to which she clutched the duster.

> *O, amore misterioso*
> *Misterioso altero*
> *Croce*
> *Croce e delizia*
> *Croce e delizia*
> *Delizia al cuore*

In the opera a rich young man falls in love with a courtesan who is beautiful and pure of heart but is considered an unacceptable object of his desires by his father because of her many affairs. After having had this aria sung to me so many times I soon came to see myself as both the cross and ecstasy of my mother's life. Usually the cross.

Another time, I sat in my chair eating a piece of cheese she had given me to nibble on as she showed how Alfredo had flung the gambling money he had won in Violetta's face in front of all of their friends.

"Oh this is the best part," she said, acting out all the roles, soprano, baritone, and tenor for me. He thinks she left because she wanted to return to her older, wealthier lover but really it's because his father convinced Violetta that she would ruin Alfredo's life if she stayed with him. My mother clutched some Canadian dollars impersonating francs and threw them at me and said,

> *I have called you here as witnesses*
> *that I have paid her all I owe.*

Then Mama crumpled to the floor, *Violetta fainting in Flora's arms*. I gave her a standing ovation from my high chair.

with orchestral accompaniment

My earliest memory as a social being was being a flower girl at my youngest aunt's wedding. I think by the time I was ten I must have attended about a hundred weddings. If there's one thing my family likes to do, it's to get married. I was five and Mama made me a floor-length peacock-blue chiffon dress with matching gloves. Mama put my hair in little ringlets and a bun and I got my first pair of pantyhose. They were white because "nice little girls didn't wear nude pantyhose," Mama said.

There were six hundred people at this wedding and it was held in a hall near our church, All Souls. I distinctly remember three older girls standing in front of the church before the ceremony saying how cute I looked. Well I guess all the attention got to me because somehow I got it into my head that I was getting married. Since I was the star of the event I decided that I would or wouldn't do certain things.

For instance, when the small orchestra started playing I didn't want to dance with the ring boy for the first dance. Needless to say my cousin was devastated. When they wanted to take pictures in front of the fountain outside, I hid in the salon with some other cousins and spent the next hour adding salt to unguarded glasses of red wine. Over the years this evolved into the favourite sport of small children at weddings. At the end of the night I wouldn't take off my dress because I looked so good in it. I didn't want the day to be over. And when my mother finally forced me to take off this dress at three in the morning so she could get some sleep, I screamed at her that I never wanted to get married again for the rest of my life.

a form of drama

One time my brother Joey and I walked all the way to the Centre Mall to ride the kiddie cars which we had seen the day before. We walked hand in hand to the mall. It had small fire engines, trucks, convertibles, everything. And miniature stop signs with a cut out policeman holding up his white-gloved hand to stop the cars. We had neglected to tell my mother and spent an hour or so looking longingly through the wire fence at the cars because we forgot it was a Sunday and that the mall wasn't open. I thought we had only been gone for an hour.

We made our way back to the house. On the way home I bought Joey some candy strawberries and mint leaves from Turner's Variety. My mother was standing on the porch, her white knuckles gripped around the broom, her face a tomato red.

"Where have you been?" she screamed, already making her way down the steps of the porch. Joey grabbed the hem of my dress and pulled it hard, his little knees knocked together.

"I . . . we . . . "

WHACK! The bottom of the broom landed on the top of my head and then hit Joey in the back. He jumped forward and cowered a little closer to me. I pushed him away looking for cover. Of course there was none. I thought about running around the billboard that sat in front of our house but I knew it would be worse if I ran. Besides I'd have Joey dragging from my ankles.

"I said, 'Where-WHACK-were-WHACK-you-WHACK?'"

"I . . . I . . . I."

"Ayayayay, I'll give you ayayay!"

She dragged us both by one arm and pulled us into the basement. We had a wine cellar where my father kept barrels of homemade wine and preserves that my mother made each autumn. There was no electricity. It was cool and pitch black. She shoved us into the wine cellar and bolted the door from the outside.

"This will teach the both of you to wander off without telling me where you're going!"

Then we heard her stomp upstairs into the kitchen above. At first, Joey and I just sat on the concrete floor and cried quietly, trying to catch our breath. His little chest heaved up and down and his lower lip trembled. I could tell because when she pushed us Joey's head ended up on my lap. Eventually he snuggled closer and buried his six-year-old head into my dress. I was too miserable to push him away. After all it had been my idea, Joey just came along for the ride, so I let him lie there. After about ten minutes Joey started wailing again, loudly. I couldn't help it, then I started too.

So we both kept crying and calling out to her to come and let us out. We thought she couldn't hear us so we kept getting louder and louder. Later she said she was trying to teach us a lesson. She just turned up Verdi's *Macbeth* a little bit each time. Joey kept saying "Sorry, sorry, sorry" in this blubbery voice. I said "Shut up, stupid!" after a while because I was so mad.

About an hour later, we heard my father come home from the Trinacria Club, a social club for Sicilian men that he went to on Sunday afternoons. He heard the screaming from the front door. He burst into the house, slammed the door and yelled, "*Che é 'sta opera?*" My mother finished her coffee and then came down and let us out. I heard him screaming at her but she just stood there and said, "*Tutto é finito,*" like Macbeth to his wife after he stabs Duncan. That shut him up.

We spent the rest of the evening sulking in our rooms. My father was in the back yard working on the garden and my mother was in the living room. I could hear *Macbeth* coming from downstairs.

recitatives

Breakfast was the best time of the day, after Mama's shift but before she started the housework. We had to have an egg every day for breakfast. Sometimes with something but always an egg. Some days she stood humming over the stove and prepared an egg *frittata* for us. It was like a big round omelette with ricotta cheese. Or we ate soft boiled eggs. She cut thin strips of bread we dipped into the yolk. Or she slipped us an egg in our milk. We'd say, "My milk tastes funny, Ma," and she'd say, "Never mind my little chick, drink up," and plant a big kiss in the middle of our foreheads. If we were good we could have *ciambelle* or lady fingers with Nestlé's Quik.

I guess she had listened to one too many records because she started talking to the three youngest, Joey, Carla, and I, like they talked in operas between arias and choruses. These are called recitatives.

"Would you like some cer-e-al?" she sang in Italian.

"Thanks, Ma."

"With milk or creeeeam?"

"Milk, please."

"How about juuuuuice?"

"Uh, no thanks."

Carla and Joey still loved it, but after all I had been hearing it since my high-chair days. Then Joey and I bundled up and trotted off to Our Lady of Perpetual Agony, the local grade school presided over by Sister Musselle, A.K.A. Sister Mussolini.

Sometimes I'd forget and as I left I'd yell "Goodbyyyye!" and Mama would glance up with a puzzled look wondering why I was talking so strangely.

and sometimes dance

Usually we fought between ourselves so much about what shows to watch that we had to have TV days assigned. I got Monday, Wednesday, Friday. Joey got Tuesday, Thursday, Saturday, except Saturday afternoon. Nonna, our father's mother, loved wrestling so we had to watch that. Her other favourites were "Wild Kingdom" and "The Man from U.N.C.L.E." She didn't understand a word of English but she loved those shows. Sunday was "family day" which meant we had to "shut up one day of the week" and let Mama or Papa decide. Papa always watched "Tiny Talent Time" on Channel 11, produced right here in Hamilton. He said he wanted me to be on the show because I was such a great dancer, and I was.

I would close the living-room door and dance with a long chorus line of men, preferably on a ship. I could hear my mother vacuuming upstairs, my Papa would be at work, Joey was playing on the lot in front of the house. In my dance sequence, I was tall with bright red lipstick and legs up to there. I think I saw this woman, the one I was trying to imitate, on a Saturday matinee. I took my mother's lipstick and painted a big red circle on my lips. Then I got a red crayon and coloured my toes and fingernails in. I wanted to use real nail polish but I knew I wouldn't be able to destroy the evidence quickly enough.

The only thing was, I was much too shy to dance for anyone other than my father. When guests came he would tell them how wonderful I was and there I'd be wrapped inside the curtains which separated the living room from my parents' bedroom. So Papa would end up shaking me out of the curtains like a flea from a dog, trying to get me to sing and dance for the company, but I usually ran into their bedroom and hid under the bed as the adults talked and cracked walnuts and drank vermouth. After a while my Papa gave up on grooming me for a show business career.

scenery

Our neighbourhood was so nasty that the girls used to beat each other up as well as any boy who tried to intercede. Once, there was a fight in front of McDonald's and one girl in a halter top got it torn right off and she kept on fighting until a man finally pulled her aside and wrapped his jacket around her.

At Our Lady of Perpetual Agony, there was a girl named Ellen in grade eight who kicked everyone else around. She followed Joey and me one day into Turner's Variety and called him a sissy who wore girl's shoes because he was wearing little white shoes from Italy. I couldn't do anything except repeat "They're not girl's shoes!" in this squeaky voice over and over hoping she wouldn't beat us up until she finally got bored and left us alone.

But still I liked Ellen. She looked kind of like a cat with her vague grey eyes and pretty hair, maybe that's why I liked her. I embarrassed her by telling everyone one day that she was my second-best friend after Theresa. Of course the rest of her gang loved that. They followed her around the school yard and teased her until she finally threatened to kick their heads in. But sometimes if some of the other girls were bothering me she'd joke around and say they'd better leave me alone because I was her second-best friend.

One night in the summer of that year, my sister Katerina, cousin Lianna, and I were sitting in front of my house on Papa's old bronze-coloured station wagon. Our parents were in the kitchen drinking espresso and talking. I could hear the low murmur of their voices from where we sat in the street light. Ellen came by with two girls I didn't know.

"Look at the wops sitting there, greasing up that car!" one tossed over her shoulder like a discarded candy wrapper. They all laughed, even Ellen.

I recognized Ellen but she pretended she didn't know me. I looked at my cousin Lianna; she wasn't from the neighbourhood. My sister Katerina knew better, we both went to the same school. She knew all about Ellen. And her friends.

"Look at the sluts that just walked by," Lianna said loudly and lay back on the car. I saw the three heads freeze then turn around.

I slipped off the car and made my way to the house. I wanted to tell one of the parents that we were all going to be killed. I could hear slapping and scuffling. I stood at the kitchen table trying to say something but I couldn't. I knew that either my cousin was going to be killed tonight or that I was going to be killed tomorrow at school for having told. So I stood there and said nothing.

Later Lianna and Katerina came in and told our parents that the girls had tried to slap them but my cousin slapped them right back. My aunts and uncles asked me why I hadn't said anything to them about what was happening, but I just stood there, kicking the table leg until they finally got bored and resumed talking and drinking. Even Lianna and Katerina left, probably disgusted with me too.

choruses

Choruses are, in opera, as in other forms of music, a "simultaneous utterance of words, cries, etc. . . . " This perhaps explained my mother and father's "parenting style." It is also a concise summation of my teenage years.

"I'm going out now," I'd say and grab my coat to go out the kitchen door.

"She's going out now?" my father asked over his copy of *Il Corriere*.

"You're going out now?" my mother repeated. Funny about that echo in the kitchen.

"Yes."

"Now?"

"Yes. Now. It's only a few minutes after eight." I scooped a bunch of home-grown grapes into my hand and dangled them above my mouth.

"It's almost nine, you can't go out, it's too late!"

"Too late, much too late," my father said without looking at me. He turned the page of the newspaper.

She slammed the iron down onto its holder and grabbed the next set of sheets. She ironed sheets, towels, underwear, even socks. The woman had no mercy.

"I've finished my homework, done the dishes, swept the kitchen, what more do you want?" I counted off my chores on my fingers as I spoke.

"What more do I want? What more do I want?"

"Yes, what more do you want?" I asked, looking out the window for my friend Theresa who lived around the corner.

"More, that's what I want, more!" My mother stumbled over the English. She was frustrated with it because she couldn't get sufficiently angry in English. "Where are you going?"

"Yes, Lilla, tell your mother where you're going." He coughed nervously and turned the page.

"We're going to Burger King on our bikes and then . . . " It was always the hesitation that got me in trouble. "UH . . . then we'll uh just ride around . . . "

"Burger King! Ride around! No! NO! NOOOO! I need you here. Who do you think I am? Madame Butterfly waiting for Pinkerton all my life while you're up to no good?"

Once my mother mentioned Madame Butterfly my father knew I was in real trouble. He went to the living room and turned on the TV, removing himself from the line of fire. I could hear him coughing quietly.

"I need you to water the garden," she said.

"Papa did the garden."

"Then I need you to finish the ironing."

"Ma, you're almost done, what do you want me to do, iron the dish cloths?"

"Then go check on your sister Carla."

"SHE'S SLEEPING!"

"I don't care, sit in her room until she wakes up in case she calls me or wets the bed." Then she shot me "the look," the kind that every child of an Italian parent knows. The kind that burns holes in your clothes and entrails.

I knew that once again I had met defeat. I stomped upstairs and read a year-old, ripped-up copy of *True Confessions* that my cousin Lianna had given me and that I'd stashed under Carla's bed.

in which music is a dominant factor

I remember music was a big part of our life on Paradise. Not just opera but Sicilian folk music. My parents would have parties and stay up late Friday or Saturday night. The bath-tub was full of ice and beer, there were bottles of red wine in the kitchen and the stereo blared into the cool night.

After enough wine, the tables were cleared and we danced. Mama was usually the first one to start. She grabbed my Papa and clamped her hands around his waist and shoulder. After several songs they sank into their chairs, sweat gleaming on their arms and my father took out his handkerchief and wiped his forehead. He couldn't keep up with Mama. Then all my aunts and uncles and even some of the cousins started dancing. Sometimes the neighbours would call the police because the music was still playing at two or three a.m. but more often than not they'd drop by for a glass of wine and a slice of homemade pizza.

acting

That same summer of perpetual parties and get-togethers, my father was hospitalized. They found a growth on his lungs in April. Later Mama said, "I knew we were too happy." The centuries-old Sicilian cynicism crept into her voice. We visited him every night. I told him funny stories about school and Joey brought him crayoned pictures. He got me to hang them up on the wall. Carla sat on his lap and looked adorable, something I'm told she was good at.

I never knew how sick he was. If I was told, I didn't believe it. I thought Mama was doing a pretty wicked impersonation of Maria Callas in . . . anything. Her ranting and arm waving and crying. I leaned over to Joey during one of her rampages and whispered, "She should have gone on the stage . . . " only to find the back of my head miraculously meet the back of her hand. Papa told her to leave me alone, too exhausted to argue about it. I could see he badly needed a cigarette.

At home she flew into a rage if we made too much noise, wrestled, watched the TV too loud. She locked herself away in the family room every night when we came home from the hospital. She played the music of all the tragic heroines: Lucia di Lammamoor, Aida, Tosca, Anna Bolena, and of course Violetta. She sat on the back porch with a cold cup of coffee in her hands every night after the hospital. I tried to put my arms around her once.

"Leave me alone, Lilla, I don't feel like playing." She stood up and took a sip of the cold coffee. "He's going to die," she said to me. She looked over the porch into the sunset made a pretty pink and purple by the steel they were making at Stelco and Dofasco. One small tear was running down her cheek and she brushed it away, pretending it was a bit of sleep. I acted like I didn't see it.

I said to myself, "He won't die." I just never thought he would. Then I went inside and back into my room. Joey came in, scared and crying.

"She's just acting, Joey, you know Ma." I let him put his chubby arms around my shoulders, which I hardly ever did. Usually I was throwing spoons at him (which were safer than knives), making him swallow pennies or pushing him off the verandah because he was always making me mad. But just then I felt like a heroine in one of Mama's operas. Anna Bolena about to be beheaded, Desdemona smothered by Otello, or maybe Tosca pleading for her lover's life. I wrapped my arms around

Joey and closed my eyes, the sweet music of Verdi floated over me from the family room.

etc . . .

Mama sold the house on Paradise when Papa died. The music just didn't sound the same in the house after he was gone. We all thought it was kind of funny that the new house was on Upper Paradise. She moved there to be closer to her sisters. We see her every couple of weeks since we've all grown and married, even Carla the youngest got married last year. We sit around and drink a glass of wine and listen to her old opera records. We bought her a few CD's but she hates them and always makes us take them back. She loves her old records with their scratches and faded album covers. She says the scratches give them life.

ANTANAS SILEIKA

Going Native

S tan was a DP like my father, like the rest of us, but the outhouse made even him laugh. Not the outhouse itself, although it was the only one in the subdivision growing up in the old orchards, but the neat squares of newspaper my father had us stack beside the seat.

"You such a fuggen DP," Stan said to my father, and he held his sides as he laughed like a character out of a cartoon. Stan only swore when he spoke English, a language that didn't really count.

My father went out and bought two rolls of toilet paper, but for half a year we used them only as decoration, like twin flower vases. Stan's advice was reliable. As for what the Canadians advised, one could never be sure. Their way of life was strange enough. But within this strangeness were odd people – those who might advise you not from the authority of their culture, but from some kind of disturbed centre.

"A fool is always dangerous," my father told me, "but a foreign fool is worse. You can't tell if he's simply an idiot or simply a foreigner."

Mr. Taylor was the only real Canadian we knew in the dawn of our subdivision, and we watched him as if we were anthropologists trying to decipher the local customs.

Mr. Taylor was a special kind of Canadian, an "English." They were the only kind who really counted, and observation of them could pay a dividend. Mr. Taylor was *our* English, the one who lived across the street and whose habits could be observed at will. We were astonished that he kept on his dress shirt and pants as he read the evening paper in a lawn chair in his back yard. The lawn chair was just as astonishing. Who else but an English would spend good money on a chair that could only be used outside?

"These English are just like Germans," my mother sighed. We knew what that was supposed to mean – good – not DP. Only Germans and English of a certain type were not DP.

"He's a banker," my mother told us, and the word was heavy with meaning. It explained how he lived in a house that not only had proper brick walls and a roof, but a lawn as well. His was the only other house on our street, and a contractor finished his home, even though we had started first. One day we had even woken to the smell of tar, and gone out to see that he was having his driveway paved.

My father snorted at this. It was 1953. Our street was still covered in gravel and if a man had money, he laid crushed stones on his driveway. Everybody else had ruts on their yards. Asphalt was as unlikely as a skyscraper in the new suburb-to-be, where the apple trees from the old farm orchards still stood in rows all around us, their sad fruit unpicked. But Gerry and I were filled with envy. A paved driveway was a sign of sophistication – something so fine we never knew it was possible until we saw it.

"What a game of hockey you could play on this," Gerry said to me one Thursday evening when we knew the banker and his wife were out shopping, and we knelt on the pavement to feel the smoothness with the palms of our hands. "You could shoot a ball from one end of the driveway to the other, and it would almost score by itself. A ball on pavement moves faster than a puck on ice. My science teacher told me that." I listened and I palmed the smooth pavement and the vision in Gerry's mind was seeded in mine.

My older brother Gerry became the first Canadian in our family. He sensed the openings in this country faster than the rest of us, and he slipped through them. If we were quick enough, we could slip in behind him. He could outskate the fastest of them, and leave only the half-heard whisper of "ass hole" in their ears. The goalies feared him most, because the Life magazines stuffed in their socks did nothing to save their shins from the sting of his flying puck.

But to Mr. Taylor, he was only a boy, and a suspect boy at that. The kind of boy who was sure to have matches in his pocket, if not a stolen cigarette as well.

When Mr. Taylor crossed the street to speak to my father, we felt suddenly naked. He had seen us for the first time.

"Your cat," said Mr. Taylor to my father, "has been running across my lawn."

My father glanced down at Gerry and me to see if he had understood the English correctly. Gerry shrugged, and my father pondered the words.

The relationship between our cat and Mr. Taylor's lawn was impossibly remote to him. What could the one have to do with the other? My father sucked on his pipe, and the sickening sputter of nicotine resin in the stem was the only sound. Clearly there was a problem, or this English would not be there, standing in his shirt and tie in the ruts by our subterranean home. My father strained to imagine the problem.

"It shits on your lawn?"

Gerry and I were mortified. The colour rose in Mr. Taylor's face as well, for in 1953, a man did not speak that way, not out in front of his house. Gerry and I knew it, but my father did not.

"No, no," Mr. Taylor said. "That is not what I meant."

"It pisses on your flowers?"

"It merely walks. I do not want your cat to walk on my lawn."

It was all that Mr. Taylor could admit to without uttering the same sort of profanities as his neighbour. My father would never understand terms such as *defecate* or *urinate*. Mr. Taylor's linguistic squeamishness had backed him into a corner.

My father sucked on his pipe and thought some more. He had negotiated with Red Army commissars and saved his sister-in-law from a Nazi labour battalion, but he had never heard a complaint such as this. This had to be an eccentricity. Banker or not, Mr. Taylor was an idiot.

"I fix," my father said.

Mr. Taylor would have been happy to leave it at that, to take his victory against the foreigner and return to his evening paper, but my father gestured for him to stay where he was, and then went down the steps to our underground house.

He came out with the cat in his hand. He did not cradle the cat, for my father had come from a farm, and cradling was only for women or citified men. He carried the cat by a handful of skin behind its head, and he held it out to Mr. Taylor.

"I told the cat not to walk on your lawn, but it doesn't listen to me. You tell it."

The cat hung in the air, its legs splayed and tense, but its face calm and inscrutable.

Mr. Taylor's lips pursed.

"Seriously, if it walks on your lawn again, you can kill it."

Mr. Taylor stepped out of our ruts and onto the gravel street, and he walked determinedly back to his own home.

"I can kill it for you if you want. Tell me and I will do it!" He shouted at Mr. Taylor's back, but Mr. Taylor's back continued to recede.

That had been in the summer, but the memory of it must have stuck in Mr. Taylor's mind throughout the months as it became clear that our pit in the earth was never going to have a proper house on top of it before the winter snows fell. The memory of it must have galled him as it became clear that the outhouse was not going to come down either, and his revulsion must have grown when my mother brought home the baby in November.

One February morning we heard the muffled thump of a foot against the snow on the cellar door. A real distinction, the only family in Weston that had a door you knocked on with your feet.

I looked up at the building inspector from the bottom of the staircase, a dark figure against a blue so brilliant that it hurt my eyes. My father had been there first. Gerry and I came over in case we had to translate for him. Only my mother hung back by the wood stove because Tom was on her breast and the cold was always slipping down the stairway like an eager cat.

It was the wood stove that gave us away in the first place. He never would have found us after a new snow if it weren't for the smoking pipe above us. After every snowfall, my father dug out the stove-pipe so the smoke could pass freely, and from a distance you could always see the plume rising out of the ground at the top of the hill like a vent out of hell. The plume gave us away to him. That and the outhouse.

We had no doubt that the man at the top of the stairwell, the town building inspector, had been called by Mr. Taylor.

"Come in!" my father shouted heartily. "It is cold – my wife will make some tea."

My father was desperate to get the man to sit at a table. There would be no trouble then, not if he could see the inside was clean and we had a baby as well. A cup of tea at best, and a couple of drinks and ten dollars at worst would get rid of the problem. But the inspector would not come down the steps.

"The law says you can't live like this. It's not decent." He called down the stairwell as if he were looking down into the hold of a slave ship. "The roof doesn't have enough pitch, and the snow could crush every one of you!"

"Wait. My English poor."

This was another tactic in my father's strategy for life in a foreign land. He could deny he had understood anything, and an order not understood never existed in the first place.

"It's for your own good," the inspector said. We could not make out his face – he was like an angel at the top of the staircase, surrounded by painful blue light.

"We have a baby," my father said expansively, as if showing off a new heifer. He motioned to my mother and she stepped closer into the cold air that came down the steps.

"The baby'd be the first to go when the roof collapses."

"Danger?"

"For the baby. Yes. You must move out for the sake of the baby."

"Then you take the baby." My father took Tom from my mother's arms, and she did not complain, did not hesitate.

"You take the baby and bring him back in April when the snow is gone. If you like, bring him back in September, after we have the walls and the roof." A crunch of snow as the inspector left, and then a quick return.

"Are you Catholic?"

"What?"

"Your religion."

"Church of England."

The inspector slammed the door down on us.

How could my father have known there was a Catholic Children's Aid? An admission of religion would have brought them down on us. He was in seas only partially mapped, and where he was ignorant of how to act, he navigated by dead reckoning.

Dead reckoning could be a problem. Sometimes it was dead wrong, and my mother was not sure my father had his bearings right.

"You were ready to give him the baby."

"So why did you hand him to me?"

"I thought you knew what you were doing."

"I do. He won't be back."

"But what if he does come back? What if they make us leave? We have no place to go."

"I know what I'm doing."

"Just like you said we'd have the roof on by the end of September."

"We ran out of money."

She knew that. She had calculated how many nails he would need, so there would be none left over – no extra money spent for nails that would sit in a box for years later. She knew the butcher gave a free piece of liver if she bought a pound of bacon – double the savings because she could use the bacon drippings on our sandwiches instead of butter. She knew the matters of money very well – the cost of condensed milk for the baby and counting the tins of it on the shelf each day because Gerry might snatch one and suck it dry himself.

And this problem of money was not a new one for her, because even in the house where she had lived before the war, the men who came to cut the hay were paid in eggs or meat or beer and as little money as possible. She knew the value of money even from up in the tower of the white frame house that was gently sinking into the mud below. A shallow pit had to be dug so the front door could swing open. The problem of money had always been there. She was the one who brought home fifteen cents of lamp oil each day, so her father could read to them from Shakespeare for an hour.

They were sent to bed when there was still a little oil left in the lamp, and her father stayed up alone to read Voltaire in translation. He put the book behind others when the priest came to visit. Voltaire was their secret – they knew not to talk of him or the book – it was their father's weakness, like a need for liquor or pornography. He paid for his Voltaire by reading Shakespeare to the girls. They already learned German in school – so he was edifying them, arming them with another language. It never occurred to him that any other book was necessary for their English. If he could only afford to own one book, then he wanted it to be the best.

But there was no one in that distant farm country, no one else outside the rotting wooden manor in that tiny parish, the dependency of a minor provincial town, who spoke or read a word of English. She memorized and repeated Hamlet's speech. The girls spoke to one another in Shakespeare's English at the dinner table where their mother silently watched the servant girl dish out the mashed potatoes and listened to the foreign sounds without understanding a word. Even their father had been self-taught, and so father and daughters spoke to one another, innocent of the rules of English pronunciation.

And so years later, she became the English teacher in the DP camp in Oldenburg, in the British Zone, and when the English colonel came on an inspection visit, she was the one who had trained the children and had them repeat in a chorus:

> *Now is the Winter of our discontent*
> *Made glorious summer by this son of York;*
> *And all the clouds that lower'd upon our house*
> *In the deep bosom of the ocean buried*

But the English colonel heard the rhythmic beat of foreign vowels and consonants of what he guessed was some folk poem. It was only months and years later that my mother and her now dispersed English students were bewildered in front of immigration officers on the piers of Halifax and New York and Sydney as their words made no impression on officialdom, which scowled or smiled on them depending on their luck, but which clearly understood nothing of the winter of their discontent.

Now my mother was marooned with her children in the underground dwelling, a victim of my father's dead reckoning, yet he assured her that the way ahead of us was clear. We could go on confidently until spring, when there would be enough money for the walls and a roof. If only the inspector did not return, that emissary of the English Mr. Taylor, that scuttler of our dreams. For the bank was only a hundred yards down the road from the town hall. Mr. Taylor and the inspector were practically the same man, and to make an ally of one would make an ally of the second.

"I'll bake them a Napoleon cake," my mother said, and my father approved the expenditure on three pounds of butter, two dozen eggs, and flour and vanilla.

"It would be cheaper to kill the cat. Then he'd be happy for sure."

Gerry and I looked at one another, panic stricken, but my mother just shook her head swiftly at us. It meant either that my father was joking or she wouldn't let him do it.

She chopped the butter into the flour with a knife.

"Don't let the butter get too warm, or it won't form into grains. There's another way of doing this whole thing, a method of folding over the pastry to make puffs. That's the way the French do it, and after all, this is a French cake. But we have our own special innovation, so we chop the butter into the flour until the pieces are the size of small peas."

"If we burnt his house down, we'd be rid of him sooner."

Gerry was walking around the room, rocking Tom in his arms as my mother made the cake. He looked funny to me, his face all fierce and twisted and the baby in his arms. I laughed.

"Don't think I wouldn't do it."

"It's a brick house. How are you going to make it catch fire?"

"Toss a bottle of gasoline through the window."

"You'd be in jail in a minute."

"They'd never catch me. I'd go north into the woods."

"Stop that talk," my mother said. "You're beginning to sound like your father."

That shut us up.

"Then you roll out each leaf right on a round metal pan. Don't try to lift the rolled leaf from the counter onto the pan because it has to be thinner than a pie crust, and it'll break as you move it."

Our basement room was sweltering with the heat from the wood stove. Gerry and I were in our T-shirts.

"You have to be just as careful when you take the leaf out. It's supposed to be very thin. And you need at least twelve of these leaves. If one does break, crumble it up and use it as a garnish on the very top layer."

"What are you telling us this for?" Gerry asked. "We're never going to bake cakes."

"I don't have any daughters."

"Well I'm not going to be one for you."

"You look like one already with that baby on your arms," I said.

"You take him. Catch!"

"Toss that child and you will not be able to sit down for a week, I promise you."

Gerry scowled.

"Make a custard with sugar and a dozen egg yolks and a little milk," my mother said. "Then make sure you let the custard cool, because if you add butter to hot custard, it will melt and separate. Beat the butter into the custard, and spread a little between each of the leaves."

"I said I'm never going to bake one of these."

"This is a Napoleon cake. Do you know who Napoleon was?"

"Yeah," Gerry answered, but he did not sound sure of himself.

"He was a French general who became the most war-like man France has ever known. He knew how to use artillery – big guns – and he marched across most of Europe. This cake is named for him."

"But I bet he didn't bake it himself."

"Don't be so sure. Napoleon was a man who knew all weapons."

After Gerry suggested we put a dead mouse in the middle of

the cake, my mother selected me to take the gift across to the banker and his wife.

The beaten snow path to the road was slippery, and half an inch of water lay on the icy road. We were in the middle of a warm spell, and icicles hung off the eaves and the sound of running water came from under the snow. The cake was heavy, placed on a board covered with wax paper, and I had to hold it out in front of me with two hands.

Mrs. Taylor answered the door.

My mother had made me rehearse the whole speech twice, about neighbours and friendliness and helping out, but I froze when I saw her in her perfection. Short hair, red lipstick (lipstick at home!) and a dress with short sleeves and cuffs and a blue-checked apron. She looked like she had stepped out of an ad in the household section of the Eaton's catalogue.

"You're beautiful!" I said, and then regretted it, and felt ashamed of the grey wool mittens that she could see holding up the cake. They were scratchy, like everything else I had to wear in the wintertime, but worse they were wet and had a patch where I'd poked my finger through once and my mother had repaired it with pink thread. Pink thread and grey mittens came from across the road, in the basement where we lived, and I hoped then that we *would* be forced to move, because I couldn't bear the shame of being across the road from her.

Mrs. Taylor laughed, and asked me what I had in my hands.

"A cake. We baked it for you."

Mr. Taylor was behind her in a moment.

"We can't take that."

"Oh, Harvey, they're just trying to be nice."

"It might not be sanitary."

"Hush. Thank you, dear, and say thanks to your mother. Wait a minute," and she disappeared back into the house.

Mr. Taylor stood there glowering at me, and I looked down and away from him, and studied the lower walls of his house, where the concrete blocks came out from the ground to meet the bricks. There was a step-shaped crack there and I stared at it until Mrs. Taylor came back.

"There's a piece of fudge for you and one for your brother.

Now remember to thank your mother." I took the two pieces, each wrapped in a square of wax paper, and stuffed them into my pocket and went back home.

"Thank God for women," said my mother as she nursed Tom in the armchair.

"You say they had a crack in the basement wall?" my brother asked.

"Yeah."

"We could pour acid through there and it'd turn into gas. We could poison them."

"A boy exactly like his father."

The uncharacteristic February thaw kept up with much dripping of icicles and gurgling in ditches still covered with snow. Three days later, the temperature dropped to zero and the neighbourhood became a treacherously shiny surface. Gerry and I skated over the crust of ice that had formed on the snow in the abandoned fields beyond our subdivision. He could always last longer than me, and he came in one night after dark, when the rest of us were already finishing our supper at the kitchen table. He was carrying a strange bundle of newspapers that he pulled apart before anyone could say a word. The Napoleon cake fell from the newspaper wrapping and clanged onto the floor like a piece of iron.

It was frozen from sitting outside. No piece had ever been cut from the cake.

"Where did you get that?" my father asked.

"It was wrapped up in newspapers in their garbage can. I thought you wouldn't believe me if I told you about it, so I dug it out and brought it home."

"Did they see you?" my father asked.

"They're out shopping."

"What do you think people will say about us if they find out you've been lifting the lids off garbage cans?" my mother began, but my father cut her off.

"He did the right thing. Now at least we know where we stand."

"I've got a plan, Dad," said Gerry, and my father turned to him to listen. Gerry had just earned the right to speak.

"There's a crack in their basement wall. Dave saw it. We get some kind of acid, you know, something poisonous, and we pour it through the crack, and then at night the fumes rise up through the house and kill them both."

My father sucked on his unlit pipe, and the nicotine in the stem made the sickening slurping sound.

"What crack?"

"The crack in their basement wall."

"Did you see it?"

"Yeah, I checked it. We could get this little pipe or something and do it at night. We'd just have to cover our tracks in the snow and nobody'd be the wiser."

"You say they are out shopping?"

"They go every Thursday."

"And you could show me this hole?"

Gerry couldn't believe my father was taking him seriously. He was getting more and more excited, stepping from side to side in the puddles from the melted snow on the concrete floor.

"Why are you letting him go on like that?" my mother asked. "He's morbid enough as it is."

"I want to see this hole," my father said, and he rose deliberately from his chair and carefully stuffed his pipe before going to put on his coat and hat.

Gerry looked back triumphantly at my mother and me before the two of them took the steps up and out of the cellar.

"Are they going to kill them?" I asked her.

"Nothing would surprise me from your father, nothing at all."

"You mean he'd do it?"

"What?"

"Kill them."

"He can't even bear to prune a tree. He's all talk, talk, talk, and it all winds up being no more significant than farting in the bathtub."

I didn't like it when she spoke like that. She had told me again and again about the house with a tower, and her childhood there with a view over the fields and woods. A woman from a white house should not talk about farts.

That night, Gerry whispered to me in the bed.

"We're on," he said.

"You mean you're going to kill them?"

"Father said the crack was big enough to slip a straw through."

I had visions of Mrs. Taylor in her apron, falling to her knees in the kitchen as the poisonous fumes rose up. She'd be at the stove, frying fish sticks, and when she fell unconscious, the grease would catch fire, take hold on the curtains, and soon she'd be surrounded by flames. Mr. Taylor's cigarette would fall from his mouth as he was reading the newspaper. If I watched the house carefully, I could break through the door just at that moment and carry her out to the back yard. I thought about her size for a moment, and then decided I could drag her if I had to. By then it would be too late to save Mr. Taylor, and when she woke from unconsciousness, she would wrap her arms around my shoulders and cry.

The imminent destruction of the Taylors was beginning to seem less appalling.

We were sitting down to dinner the next day when my father came in from work.

"The neighbours are taken care of," he said, and immediately sat at the table and began to slurp on his soup.

Gerry and I froze.

"You mean you did it without me?" Gerry asked.

"Of course. This was no business for a boy."

Gerry slammed his spoon down on the table. I wondered if there was still time to save Mrs. Taylor from the flames.

"I walked over there as soon as I came home. The man keeps banker's hours, you know, so he was already in his slippers. Getting him outside was like dragging a goat by the horns, but he finally did it and I showed him the crack. Three days of thaw, I said, and already your foundation has heaved and started to crack. Wait until the real thaw comes, and then the crack will open up some more. Bad footings, I told him. To fix the foundations, he would have to dig up the whole front again. Well, he started to tell me his contractor would come back and do it, but I know a man who worked for that contractor. He's bankrupt. Mr. Taylor is going to have to pay oh, I don't know, maybe six hundred dollars to have the job done, and he doesn't have the money."

"He told you that?"

"I can tell. The house smells of liver and onions. He'll have to save to have it done. It should take him a year or two to get the money. Unless the building inspector catches sight of it and makes him do it right away."

She put her hand on his arm and she began to laugh.

Gerry was glum at the rink that night, and got into two fights. On the way home, he finally said, "I don't like it. It's not a sure thing. If that inspector shows up at our house again, I'm going to do it myself."

"Where'll you get the poison?"

"There'll be some in the science cabinet in school."

We waited over the weeks that followed, as the first heavy thaw came in March, and just as my father had said, the crack in Mr. Taylor's basement wall grew wider.

By April, we had lumber stacked in the muddy back yard, and several squares of bricks. My father whistled often and my mother took Tom out to be in the sun during the occasional warm day. Deprived of ice hockey and a murder, and not yet able to play baseball on the muddy fields, only Gerry sulked that spring in Weston when my father had finally worked out the native customs.

ROGER BURFORD MASON

The Rat-Catcher's Kiss

The pale smoke of evening fires rose straight through the beeches and elms on the heights above the small town, where *vandervogel*, wandering birds, itinerants like himself, were making their supper.

He lay back against the tree and counted the plumes. There would be the scissor-grinder, the pot-mender, the barber-surgeon, and the hurdy-gurdy man. One would be the campfire of the long-song seller; another the huckster's, with his cards of pins, and coloured ribbons, and French lace. There would be the pardoner with his bag of saints' bones, whose power would ward off the evil eye and guarantee good harvests, and nearby, for they travelled together, though they never spoke, the potion seller with his extract of dog-rose for passion, and his tinctures of marigold, bugloss, and heart's ease – all to mend broken bones, salve sores, and cure the dropsical flux.

But his was the only rat-catcher's fire.

He took bread from his bag, and an onion, which he peeled and quartered with a long-bladed knife. "Here, Mak."

The dog came running to him from the undergrowth, scrambling over his spread legs to lick his face. He threw a heel of bread onto the ground beyond his boots. Instantly, the dog leapt from his lap and fell on the bread.

"Eat slowly, dog," he said. "Consider when you may next eat." He tore off a handful of bread from the loaf and wrapped it around one of the onion quarters. "I shall eat onion tonight," he said to the dog, "since I won't be kissing any fine ladies!"

93

That, and many other observations, the rat-catcher made to his dog, before he unrolled his blanket and settled to sleep beside the dying embers of his fire.

The first thing he saw when he opened his eyes was the morning star, its point of brilliance pinned to the lightening sky. He rubbed his eyes and ran his hand over his hair, wet with dew. He rolled over onto his stomach and rested his chin on his arm.

Across the valley, columns of thin smoke rose through the trees from the morning fires of travellers like he, who would go down into the town soon, with their wares, their tricks, and their gaudy, babbling language.

He wrapped the blanket around his shoulders, and pushed into the scrub for dry tinder. He found an old nest in a rhododendron bush, and took dry leaves from where they had blown into a hollow under tangled roots, and carried them back to his camp.

He took his firebox from his bag. From long habit, his thumb found the dull depression of a musket ball, fired at him in the Pope's wars at Avignon. Caressing the dent absently, he smiled, for memory. Not in wind, nor in rain, neither night nor day, had his firebox ever failed him – no, not even in the July snow which fell at Avignon that year, whose white revenge had taught the Pope's sun-enchanted mercenaries to fear the warriors from the cold north, who had swept down upon them with swords tempered in flame and ice.

He crouched on his haunches and cocked the lightly-balanced lever of the tinderbox and put it on the ground. He took the nest and unravelled some moss and bird's down from it, and dropped them over the firing pin. Bending, he steadied the box with his left hand, and touched off the firing pin with the tip of his index finger.

There was nothing but a metallic click as the hammer struck the flint, but it brought the dog running from the undergrowth to sit with his head inclined, watching the tiny wisp of smoke rise from the leaf-litter. In a moment, licks of flame began to consume the tinder, and the dried leaves the rat-catcher threw over the burning moss, and the twigs he threw on top of the moss.

"And what will you do?" the rat-catcher said with a smile, scratching the dog's head. The dog looked intently at the rat-catcher, who looked back with amused concentration.

"So be it," he said after a moment. Without a sound the dog disappeared into the brush.

The rat-catcher put some more twigs on the fire and went in search of a dry branch to break. When he returned with an armful of broken timber, the dog was sitting by the fire with a rabbit between his paws.

"Aye," the rat-catcher said. "You did your share."

The dog's tail wagged furiously as the rat-catcher picked up the rabbit by a leg. The dog following, he went off into the brush to gut and skin the rabbit, away from the campfire.

"Heart and lights for a strong constitution," he said, throwing the dog the small organs he had delicately separated with his knife from the slather of blood and guts. He cut and broke off the two fleshy hind quarters, and threw the rest of the carcass to the dog.

"We never ate better on the plains of the Romagna," he said to the dog. "Nor yet in the mountains of Spain." But the dog paid him no attention, for he had heard these things before, whereas the rabbit was freshly killed.

The rat-catcher peeled and slit the skin of the rabbit's legs and threaded them on the end of green sticks which he leaned over the coals of his fire to roast, and while they were cooking, he went to the little stream which bubbled out of the hillside and trickled down to the valley below, to join the great river on its voyage to the north, where the sea crashed on a lonely, rocky shore.

He had seen the sea, fighting in Lepanto, and in his travels in Spain, and he loved the stories he had heard in its roar, and its terrible energy as it struggled in the moon's thrall. But he loved, too, the secret streams he knew from his travelling, the long, slow rivers that wound through flat meadows, and the torrents of white, raging water which tumbled through mountain gaps and leapt over precipices into boiling black cauldrons where the spirits of dreams and nightmares lay waiting.

He knelt and rinsed the rabbit's blood from his hands and then drank long, and rinsed his face and neck, and finally lifted handfuls of water to his tangled hair.

"Drink now," he said to the dog.

The shadow of the cathedral spire fell across the square where the rat-catcher sat, looking up at the clock. Entering the town, he had heard the hurdy-gurdy man playing his one-legged organ, and the excited cries of children who had gathered around him to dance and sing. He had passed the scissor-grinder at a street corner, sharpening knives and scissors, and the potion-seller, bragging to young maids and housewives, who listened sceptically, and laughed scornfully, at his magical flummery and outlandish claims. And where the potion-seller was, close-by he knew would be the pardoner, selling Saint Gerald's thumbbone to ward off lightning, or Saint Eligius' finger-nail to make cows calve.

"Rats?" The citizen laughed at his question. "Why, there will always be rats to catch. The town is full of them!" He pushed his hood back off his head and scratched his brow. "An' you be good, I'll pay well to be rid of the rats in my granary."

It was late in the afternoon when the rat-catcher returned to the square from the granary, where he had left one hundred and thirteen dead rats on the granary floor and the corn-merchant sweeping the bodies into a sack.

"Don't be caught sleeping out at night," had been the corn-merchant's last advice to him as he left the granary. "We whip vagrants and vagabonds from the town."

The rat-catcher listened as the heavy bell rang four times, chimes that seemed to hang in the air, one overlapping the other until the air itself throbbed. Its last note had hardly dissipated when the cathedral bells themselves began to ring, and, in a moment, black-cowled housewives, young maids, and small boys and girls began crossing the square to the cathedral doors.

"Excuse me, neighbour." His voice stopped her as she walked by him. "Do you know where I may find lodgings?"

She looked at him cautiously. "I am going to hear mass," she said. She had a low, musical voice.

He smiled. "Then I'm sorry to detain you," he said. "But I wouldn't be whipped from this fine town for a vagabond!"

She looked at him critically, but not with hostility. "I wonder you will not go?"

He smiled and shook his head. "I am not of your faith," he said.

She seemed to make her mind up quickly. "Can you pay?"

He nodded.

"Wait for me, then," she said.

He followed her through the narrow streets which led away from the square, observing her thick, black hair, now she had removed her cowl, and her straight back and strong hips. She was as tall as he, and her face, he saw when she slipped back the cowl, though not especially attractive, was evenly featured, and as unblemished as his own by the ravages of the pox, the weeping eye, or the king's evil, whose scars are the birthright of the poor.

So he was not surprised when she turned a key in the door of a substantial house, set back within a low stockade, with no house nearer than twenty yards, and them not hovels, but good substantial houses like her own.

"You'll take the room in the back, beside the bake-house," she said, leading him in the dark through a narrow, unwindowed corridor. She opened a plain wooden door. It was a small room with no window where the only furniture was a wooden box at the end of a truckle bed. "And you'll pay me at this time each day," she said, "until I get to know and trust you."

He drew the string of a small leather purse and held out some coins to her. "But I trust you already," he said with a smile. "And I know you will only take what will be fair to us both."

She looked into his smiling eyes with her grave ones and then at his spread hand with the coins in it. "This will be your rent, then," she said, taking several copper coins. "For it, you shall have breakfast too, and eat with me in the evening, if you wish."

He considered her words. "You, alone?"

She looked steadily at him, reading his unspoken inquiry.

"Alone," she said, defiantly. "My man is sergeant of halberdiers in Graf Michael's army. He is at the wars in Artois, in France."

The rat-catcher nodded. "The fine officer's house," he said, his wave taking in all they could see of the house from where they stood.

Now she smiled. "The fine house because he has fine lands and good stock," she said. "And the commission in Graf Michael's regiment because of them, too."

He nodded again, and thought of the sergeants he had known, primping, simpering men in flounces and lace who scorned to soil their hands by picking up a halberd, or risk their blood by touching a thumb to a honed edge. Her man would not be one of them, he guessed, but a solid yeoman who had made his wealth by wise economies and careful purchases. He had known his kind too, and they no more respected the lumpen soldiery – filthy, egregiously violent and lustful, dull beasts that they were – than the vapid young nobles did, who thought nothing of sending three men to their death across dangerous territory to secure a flask of wine or to steal a plump capon for supper.

"I was a soldier too," he said. He pulled up the sleeve of his tunic and showed her the livid scar which ran the length of his left forearm. "I took this when we broke the siege at Limburg."

She touched the scar lightly, felt it as a raised weal across his brown, muscled arm. "So it was ever," she said, turning in the doorway of the dark room. "I'll make the supper."

He wiped his knife between his thumb and forefinger, licked his fingers clean, and slipped the knife into its sheath beneath his tunic. She sat watching him from the fireplace seat, kneading bread dough. He pushed his bowl away and drew the mug of ale nearer to him.

"Will you not take ale with me?"

She shook her head as she kneaded. He saw sweat glistening on her brow.

"What work do you do?" she said.

He looked at her over the rim of the mug. "Rattenfanger," he said, using the word of her language.

A slight shudder – the disgust in her soul – and the barest thinning of her lips, betrayed her feelings.

"Aye," he said. "It's not a pretty trade, I'll warrant. But a man must earn his bread, and I know how to kill."

"I'm sorry," she said quietly, "for I have no cause to denigrate your trade. I'm sure you're as necessary as the baker and the tallow-candle maker."

He nodded. "But not as wholesome," he said with a smile.

She glanced quickly at him. "We have them in the root cellar," she said. "My heart sickens every time I catch sight of one."

He thought of the turnips he had just eaten, of her horror, descending the ladder to the earthen vault below the house where the turnips and beets were stored, cool and dry, and he knew that the rats could smell her fear.

"Then I'll catch him," he said, with a laugh. "For who would share his house with a rat, if he had the skill to catch it?"

He jiggled his foot and immediately the dog was around his knees. He lifted it into his lap and spoke a few words into its ear. Then he hoisted it under his arm and carried it to the door of the root cellar.

The ladder was on ropes and pulleys to allow it to be drawn up so that the rats could not climb it into the house. He loosened the rope and lowered the ladder. Straight away, the dog bounded down into the darkness.

The rat-catcher returned to the table.

"What is your name?" he said, taking up his ale.

She looked out of the fire-corner at him. "Margaret," she said. "Margaret Tod. And what should I call you?"

"Gorpin," he said.

She frowned at the strangeness of it.

"Gorpin the scholar's son." He spoke as if reciting a litany. "Gorpin the fool. Gorpin the runaway. Corporal Gorpin of the quick sword." He put his mug down. "Gorpin of the ten wounds. Gorpin the wanderer." He laughed. "And now, Gorpin the rat-catcher."

She tested its sound. "That's not a name of ours?"

"No." He shook his head. "Not of your people."

"Where is it a man's name?"

He thought for a moment. "It was my name in the monastery of Santiago," he said. "In the hills of Umbria and the valleys of Normandy they called me Gorpin. I was Gorpin in the Welsh Marches, and by the waters of the Danube, in the barracks of the Russian Czar, and in the taverns of the Carpathian princes." He smiled and spread his hands. "Everywhere and anywhere, I am Gorpin," he said, and then added as an afterthought, "Or what you will."

She wanted to ask him more, but at that moment Mak scrambled up the ladder and into the room with a rat held lightly in his jaws. He went straight to Gorpin, who took the rat.

"Good dog," he said, ruffling the dog's neck and ears with his free hand. He sat up in his chair and brought the rat up to the level of the table. It was alive and unhurt, watching his face without moving, though its whiskers flickered constantly as if it were divining its fate from minute changes in the atmosphere of the room.

"Kill it," she gasped, horrified. "I shall be sick."

He put the rat on the table before him. "You shall not be sick," he said. "And I shall do better than kill it, I will make it leave your house, with all of its kind."

"Kill it!" she screamed. "Kill the dirty thing!"

Gorpin slowly opened his hand until he was not holding the rat at all.

"Kill it!" she pleaded, dropping her face into her hands. "Oh please, kill it!"

The rat remained motionless, but Gorpin slid down in his chair until his eyes and the rat's were level. He spoke softly to it, and made kissing sounds with his tongue under his teeth.

"Kill it," she said into her hands.

"Watch!" he replied in a commanding whisper. She pressed her face into her hands and silence filled the room, close and dark, but after a moment, despite her revulsion, she took her hands away from her face and looked.

Gorpin was slowly raising his index finger in the air before the rat's eyes, and just as slowly, like a curl of shaved wood uncoiling, the rat rose on its hind legs until it was standing perfectly straight, perfectly still, perfectly balanced. Gorpin held it suspended with his raised finger while he whispered to it, a rhythmic, chanting sibilance to which the rat paid rapt attention. And then, suddenly, his hand shot out and seized the rat again.

Her hand flew to her mouth instinctively as he raised the rat to his lips briefly. He kissed the top of its head and strode to the ladder. "Do it, now," he said.

The rat regarded Gorpin for a moment and then turned on the stairs and ran down into the darkness.

Gorpin went to the woman, who sat speechless with loathing and disgust. "Watch," he said, touching her arm. "Watch." He crouched beside her where she sat on a stool in the fire-corner, and took her cold hand in his. In a moment they heard a pattering sound, like raindrops on leaves. The rat reappeared at the head of the ladder. Mak's ears pricked up but he did not move, as the rat, and eleven others, larger and smaller, crossed from the ladder to the wall and jumped to the ledge of the open window, and from there down into the yard.

Gorpin helped Margaret rise from the stool and ushered her to the window, where she watched the rats file across the yard and disappear around the side of the barn.

"Are they gone?" she whispered at last.

He nodded. "Never to return," he said.

Leaving her at the window, he sat at the table again, and poured ale from the pitcher into his mug.

She turned from the window and her face was drained of colour. "How is it done?" she said.

He considered, his head on one side, as the dog's was often when he spoke to it.

"You must not hold hate in your heart for anything," he replied after a moment. "With love, all things are possible."

She looked out of the window.

"Your dog never barks," she said.

Margaret Tod became proud of the rat-catcher who lived at her house. After he had rid her of the rats in her root cellar she lost no time in securing him work for she told her neighbours of his skill, though she never mentioned what she had seen him do for fear he would be taken as a witch, or something damnable, and put to the test. She had seen women drowned, or buried alive and suffocated, to prove their innocence; she had seen men whipped with ropes of burning pitch, or piled with hot cannon balls, to make them confess.

In three days he caught and killed sixty rats in the town slaughterhouse; another thirty-seven in one day at the gristmill; more than twenty in the cellars beneath the convent of Our Lady, Queen of Heaven; and uncounted dozens in citizens' houses throughout the town. But despite what he had told Margaret could be done with love, Gorpin killed every rat he caught, for that was what he was paid to do.

"But how could you," she asked him once, "when your heart is filled with love for all things?"

"I kill them with a loving heart," he replied, without smiling. "And every soldier I ever killed too," he added. "All with a loving heart."

One summer evening he came home from the weaving lofts where a thousand rats had made their nests and pathways among bales of broadcloth from Brabant, Irish linen, and worsted from the hills of western England.

"You have a friend," she said sharply, as he sat to his supper.

He looked quizzically at her. "I hope I have many," he said.

"Reba," she said, "the reeve's daughter. They tell me you walk with her in the evening."

He looked at her with still eyes and what she saw caused her to glance away.

"Then they tell the truth," he said, "for the reeve is paying me five hundred thaler to rid him of the rats, and his daughter brings me my lunch and helps me to remove the dead rats, and I walk home with her in the evenings."

She sat with her back to him on the stool in the fire-corner. "Ha! And you only walk to her house?" she said bitterly.

He willed her to look at him. "When the road the wanderer would follow is blocked with snow," he said gently, "he must take another, though it may not lead where he most wishes to go."

She looked up, a long, honest look which he read in his heart. "Take care," was all she said. "All hearts are not full of love for you."

"But some are," he said.

She said nothing and after a few moments he got up and went out.

"Read me this," she said another night when he had finished his supper. She put a folded parchment down beside his plate.

"You do not read?"

She shook her head. "What woman knows that?" she said.

He turned the heavy parchment over. On the back, where the folds met, it was sealed with red wax, embossed with a boar's head. He indicated the seal. "This may be from your husband."

She touched the seal lightly. "Read it," she said. "I cannot myself, and what he says I'd as leave you told me as anyone else."

He cracked the seal and lay the parchment flat, smoothing it with a pass of his hand.

"Read it," she encouraged him, but first he skimmed it through for himself, to know what it was he had to read.

It was not from her husband but a letter from his regiment to tell her that he had been killed in the wars. The letter had taken seven months to arrive. Margaret Tod had been a widow for seven months. He walked to the window, to have light to read by, and she heard the letter without a word. When he had finished, he folded the parchment and put it into her hand. He stood behind her as she stood beside the table, motionless.

"Weep," he urged. "Ease your soul."

But she could not. She held the letter up as if she would reinterpret its ink marks, its words, the message which made her heart forlorn. "What am I now?" she whispered to the dancing figures on the page. "A plain, fat widow."

He touched her shoulder and she turned towards him.

"A plain, fat widow," she repeated, and suddenly she was weeping on his shoulder.

He stroked her back, and her long, black hair, and felt her sobs in his body. "You will be loved," he whispered. "You will be loved." He kissed her neck, and hurried to his room.

In her room, in the darkened house, she lay awake for most of the night, wondering at the warmth that had suffused her body after the rat-catcher's kiss, and in the morning, she woke, smiling.

It took a month for Gorpin and his dog to rid the reeve's weaving lofts of their thousand rats, and when he had finished, he walked with Reba to the reeve's house, to collect his fee.

"Five hundred thaler?" the reeve said with a laugh. "I'm sure I never promised you the half of that, nor the quarter."

He looked at his daughter, at her thickening waist and plump cheeks. "I think you have taken enough from me for your troubles," he said coldly. "Here's fifty thaler. Take it, and begone by tomorrow, or I'll have you whipped from the town by the constable and his men."

Gorpin looked long at the coins in his hand as anger swept over him and burned momentarily in his eyes, but then he passed his hand over his eyes and after that they were blank, unfathomable wells.

"You have the advantage of me," he said with a sudden laugh, "and there's nothing I can do but acknowledge defeat."

The reeve, who had seen the moment of anger in the rat-catcher's eyes, laughed with relief and submitted when the rat-catcher clasped him by the shoulders and planted a kiss on his cheek.

"I'll be gone, never fear."

Margaret protested, when she saw him packing his bag. He told her of the reeve's threat.

"Stay here," she said, grasping his hand. "The reeve will not dare harm you."

But he felt the urge to travel, he explained. He had already been longer at her house than anywhere for ten years or more. "Now the swallows are gathering along the eaves," he explained. "And every day, the geese fly overhead, going south."

Neighbour Bouldt, who owned the flour mill and the gristmill and was spoken of as the next reeve, appeared at the window. "Will you walk, Mistress Tod?" he asked diffidently.

Standing with her back to the window, her body was between Bouldt and the rat-catcher, who took her hand, pressed her palm, and kissed her finger tips.

"Go, walk, Margaret," he said. "You will be loved."

A cold moon silvered the rooftops of the town and the broad river flowing in the valley below. Gorpin stopped, and put his arm around Reba's shoulder. Silent Mak sat patiently at their feet.

"It will be a hard road," he said.

She nodded. "But not as hard as the road I trod at my father's house." She patted her belly. "And I shall have company, whatever may follow."

He laughed. "You will never lack company," he said.

This, then, is the truth.

Most of the rats were killed, but not all of them.

The children of the town did not disappear into a cave in the side of the hill. Only the reeve's daughter was lost, and she followed the rat-catcher about the world, and gave him children, and lived happily.

It was five hundred thaler, not fifty thousand, that the reeve agreed to pay the rat-catcher to kill all the rats, though it is true that the reeve paid the rat-catcher only fifty.

Nowhere does it mention that the reeve woke up the day after he had cheated the rat-catcher with a red rash on his cheek, nor that he bore it for the rest of his life.

And there was no little crippled boy.

He was a complete fiction.

KATHRYN WOODWARD

Of Marranos and Gilded Angels

In January 1940, on a Wednesday morning at 11:35, Erich and Irene Winter arrived in New York aboard the English liner, *Siluria*. Snow blurred the famous skyline. A sharp wind blew. It was bitter cold, yet everyone was on deck as if fearful to jeopardize the arrival by remaining below. A dark mass of overcoats lined the railing. The coats promoted an illusion of homogeneity to a passenger list that, if read more carefully, revealed a polyglot, refugees from many lands jumbled together with those merely inconvenienced by the war. But even people who are *returning* worry if they will ever touch land again. Erich, who was not *returning,* could be forgiven then if on the voyage, surrounded by nothing but the sea, he felt he would float forever. One night at dinner he expressed this aloud. Only his wife, Irene, noticed the desperation in his voice. The others at the table looked up in horror. Unaccustomed to metaphysical discussions with their meals, they had murmured evasions, *Surely not . . .* , *The thought . . .* , (disproving, Irene noted, the long-established theory of action begetting equal reaction) before returning to their soup. Now these dinner companions too stood anxiously at the railing, while below them men shouted and strained, machinery groaned, thick ropes snaked like tentacles before being pulled taut. *Isn't it wonderful*, burbled a woman in a long fur coat, *all this fuss and bother just to get us off*. Those who could hear her smiled indulgently. Erich, who stood only two away – there was a tall man between them who was hatless despite the weather – was not one of these. Erich, his gloved hand tight upon the rail, stared straight into the falling snow and wept.

Soundless tears, as if someone had adjusted the volume. Private tears. Dignified, meant for himself alone, not an attempt to attract attention. Except that such inattention was impossible given human nature and the crush of passengers at the railing. The hatless American standing at Erich's left assumed them to be tears of joy at landing in such a fine and free country, or in the very least relief. They made the American feel smug and a bit teary himself. But he was wrong, because Americans, who know everything about ingenuity and the pursuit of happiness, know nothing of such grief. The tears dripped in order to Erich's overcoat, making two wet patches in the wool. At another time and place – and of someone else – Irene would have remarked upon the patches as a form of stigmata, and the two would have smiled at one another. Weeping was not typical of Erich's displays. Exuberance, yes. Erich liked to wave his arms and shout with the best of them. He applauded wildly. He loved yelling *Bravo!* Upon hearing certain music (and in the last few years when observing daily life) he could become melancholic, even maudlin. But Irene had seen him cry only once.

"*Vergiß nicht, Erich,*" she whispered, "*das Du ein guter Mensch bist.*" She had pocketed her hands against the cold. She did not remove them to reach out and touch her husband because she respected seclusion, even between people as effectively married as she and Erich. If Erich needed her he could turn his head and be enveloped by the reassurance of her breath. If he chose to he could feel tangible proof of her presence, her left side pressed against his right. Irene believed in tangibility, in the eventual quantification of the universe. She was that type of scientist. She denied both gods and religion, but conceded to the existence of a soul for want of a better word, endowing it with the same characteristics as any organ, gland, joint, white matter, major system, tiny cell, the soul vulnerable like each of these to injury and like them mended by isolation and bed rest.

The woman on the other side of Irene noticed the tears as

well. She leaned closer, if that was possible in this crush, her breath hot against Irene's ear. "We are also grateful to be here," she said in German.

But when Irene looked up at her the woman felt the force of a wind colder than the one blowing off the river. She shrank back against her own husband, leaving a gap at the rail, wondering suddenly, panicking a bit, if their own cause, hers and her husband's, might be advanced by, might even need, such a show of tears. (It did not.)

A few minutes later the disembarking began. The two couples separated forever. Irene and Erich passed through Immigration and were met on the other side by friends.

The Winters were young and well-educated. They perfected their English with the aid of a German–English dictionary they brought with them in their luggage, fearing that such a reference work would be unavailable in America. After some false starts they found good work, Erich in a firm that ironically made money from the war, Irene at NYU. They prospered. They moved into a decent apartment. After the war they bought a car. On Sundays Erich would drive out of the city in search of peace. He took long walks on country roads. Occasionally he would discover a unbarricaded path, free of No Trespassing signs, and reach a pool of icy water, or if he was lucky the brim of a hill. *I have just come back from one of my strolls*, he would say on Sunday evening to one of his friends. He used the word, *stroll*, deliberately, claiming that, *Here no one knows how to walk*. Sometimes he said this bitterly, but not often. To his business associates he was known as a cheerful man who hiked an amazing fifteen blocks every day to work and refused to move with them to the suburbs. They smiled to themselves about the outsized fedoras he wore, guessing shrewdly that he used them to add to his height, to make him stand taller than his wife, whose own hats were always flat and saucer-like. Without asking they anglicized his name to Eric Winter, thinking they did him a favour. *You don't want to be thought of as a foreigner*, they said, and during the war Erich didn't. But these men never saw Erich outside the office, never socialized with him, never shared with him more than the occasional lunch or business dinner. They did not notice that the Americanization of Erich Winter reached a dead end at his name. By the end of the decade Erich and Irene had already returned twice to Europe.

They began with a modest two weeks in England but soon graduated to a yearly month abroad, then to two months. Irene had the summers off and Erich would neglect his business to go on these journeys taking the corresponding cut in remuneration. As the time for leaving approached Erich would grow increasingly obsessed. Always one for ideas, a man who left the details for others, he suddenly took on the meticulousness of the elderly charting the rest of their lives – every moment, like every penny, accounted for, nothing left to chance. He purchased guidebooks and travelogues, sent for street maps, plotted railway lines and mountain passes, demanded. *Dear Sir, (Kindly) send me by return post . . .* By the time he and Irene boarded their ship, or in the fifties, their airplane, Erich knew exactly where they would go, what towns they would visit, what routes they would take, what sites they would see. He left little to whim, although once, visiting a large city, he thought himself ready and taking a deep breath plunged unannounced into what had been the Jewish quarter. The experience so overwhelmed him that he took to his hotel bed for two days, unable to rise, leaving Irene the itinerary if she wanted it. (She did not.) Thereafter, he stuck strictly to cathedrals and art museums, to mountain spas, to ruins that had nothing to do with the last war. After England they toured Norway and Sweden, Greece and Italy – but not Franco's Spain – France, Belgium, Holland, Switzerland. They travelled in concentric circles whose epicentre was Germany. With each pass they inched closer and closer. In 1957 they were in Denmark, fifty miles from the German border, *Testing the waters*, Erich wrote back to their horrified friends. When they had only one day left before returning to New York their train collided with another and they perished in the wreckage. Their bodies were too badly burned to be shipped home, but their suitcases survived, battered but miraculously unopened. Their twelve-year-old daughter, whom they had promised to take on their next trip, inherited the suitcases, the apartment, a generous supply of money, and her father's home-lessness. In a few years' time she too would feel loyalty but not adherence. Possessing no pride of place, she would cross borders into a new nationality with the ease of an astral traveller. For Erich's daughter, death would become, after an initial bout of hopefulness, complete, a vacuum of total darkness. It would hold no puffy clouds, no beating wings, no promise of eternal joy. She would be rescued by her mother's no-nonsense practi-cality. She would have a happy life.

Erich had named the child, Thea. He liked the way it looked when he sketched it in his neat hand: T H E A. It had the solid permanence of a Florentine Renaissance palace. *Dear THEA*, he wrote on postcards from London, Paris, Sienna, Brussels. *This is the square where we have our morning coffee.* Irene was not par-tial to any name so long as it could not easily be degraded into a diminutive, and so long as the two of them, she and Erich, were vigilant in its pronunciation. *Tay-ya*, Irene insisted. Forcing the girl to stand up at the start of every school year and correct her teachers.

"The child has backbone," Irene (EEE-*ray*-nah, who never permitted her co-workers to call her Eye-reen), said to her friend, Irma. "She does not flinch from duty."

It was Irma Thea stayed with whenever her parents went to Europe. Irma of Erich and Irene's university days. Unlike Erich, Irma's husband had had no trouble emigrating. Five American universities vied for Emil, who was a chemist of some renown. He decided on Columbia together with two others in their cir-cle, a theoretical physicist and a mathematician. The whole group, except for Oskar Fischer, managed one way or another to escape and reassemble in New York. They suspended their sci-entific inclinations in this case to consider this (almost) whole-sale survival and subsequent reunification a miracle. It became their duty to remain close. They met frequently for dinners. They shared holidays as if they were a biological family, fol-lowing a list of overflowing tables in prescribed order: the Winters, then the Timens, the Schemels, the Blums, and so forth. Their children considered themselves nearly cousins.

Sometimes if they could get away simultaneously they vaca-
tioned en masse in converted upstate farms that catered, in the
absence of other choices, to Jews. They were a surprisingly stable group, with only one divorce. One afternoon in 1948 Irma,
red-eyed and blotchy, rang Erich and Irene's bell. Erich and Irene
installed her in their guest room until she could find a place of
her own. During this time they avoided contact with Emil (Erich
telephoned him to explain) so as not to be drawn into a family
quarrel. The moment Irma moved out, they resumed the friendship. The entire group decided unanimously that the fairest
way to deal with this split was to alternate, Emil and his new
wife one holiday, Irma the next. Before each of these festive
meals they rose, glasses in hand, and collectively toasted those
missing from such traditional family celebrations, smiling
sadly, proud of the banquet hall they would have had to hire to
hold the numbers that had not survived.

On rainy days together Irma and Thea played café. Thea placed
her two toy chairs on one side of her miniature table following
Erich's description.

We put the chairs so, he told her. *To see everything that is
happening.*

He drew a picture for Thea, a pencil sketch of the piazza,
round tables, bright umbrellas, the waiter tripping, spilling a
tray of coffee, making Thea laugh, and then he drew a special
table, larger than the others, with two chairs, together rather
than opposite, and two figures, himself easily identified by his
glasses and his exaggerated hat, Irene by the wavy hair she had
cut short that year, sitting in those chairs. Irene is frowning,
Erich tells his daughter, because it is their coffee the waiter has
spilled.

In games with Irma, Thea is the customer. Irma carries cups
of café au lait (much milk, a thimble of coffee) from the kitchen
and slices of cake. They have already travelled on the subway to
Times Square to purchase postcards so that Thea can sit at her
table, sip her coffee and write to her parents. *I am fine. How are
you?* They mail these postcards to addresses from the roster of
hotels Erich has left for them.

"So orderly, so precise," Irma commented bitterly afterwards. *July 14-20, Hotel Della Rosa, Via XX Septembre 7. Positano.* Telephone number, manager's name, room. "As if he were afraid of getting lost, of disappearing. And I remember the time he went to sit at the feet of Bruno Walter to learn about Mahler. He just stepped up to the great man's door and knocked. No letter of introduction. No note left behind for us, his friends, with the exact check-in and check-out time. He simply vanished and when he came back he told us everything he now knew about The Marrano, as your father called Mahler," her voice softening.

After each trip Thea would help Erich arrange his photographs. Thea had the job of fitting on the little black corners so that Erich could paste the photographs into an album. He took hundreds, every one peopled. Even when he wanted something scenic or a monument he included people. One imagined him prevailing on bystanders to turn around, move a little closer, smile. Sometimes Thea would come upon him bent over these albums, studying the pictures with a magnifying glass, as if they contained a hidden message. He had other albums of photographs, older ones with green marbled cardboard covers instead of the red leather he bought now, but these he kept in a cupboard in the bedroom. She had never seen him open them.

"Don't touch those," he once shouted at Thea in a rare moment of acrimony towards her.

It was a Sunday morning. She was allowed, on Sundays, to crawl into bed with her parents. The cupboard door was open.

"Why not? I want to see."

"Let's look at the other pictures instead," he said, getting up, putting on his robe. "I will show you the Campanile in San Marco. Do you know, Thea, that one day, exactly fifty years ago, the Campanile fell down? Just like that. In a tumble of bricks. Can you imagine a building just falling down?"

She could well imagine a building *just falling down*. Any child could, adding this mishap to a catalogue of previously visualized disasters: nuclear wars (cowering under their desks, backs to the windows, whenever the teacher shouted the secret word), car accidents, abandonment. Thea pictured easily her own apartment house disintegrating, dust falling into the street, she and her parents in the rubble, pots and pans, bookshelves, sofas raining down on them.

"Look, here it is today, Thea. Rebuilt, brick by brick. Just as it used to be."

Her father had a kindly face, almost a silly face, the nose too big, the eyes too dark, the shape too long. On the top perched a nest of thick and wiry hair, like something an overzealous bird might construct lest one of her chicks fall through. The hair was the colour of Thea's fountain-pen ink. Black-and-blue they called it at school, dissolving into giggles. He was an inch or so shorter than his wife.

He did not mind this but Irene found it trying. Irene was rather beautiful. She had fine, pronounced features, prominent chin, slightly bulbous eyes. The eyes made her look arousable. People noticed her, but Irene was convinced they were noting (unfavourably) the discrepancy in their heights. She did not realize how well she carried herself, straighter, prouder, more disciplined than Americans who had grown lax in their classless society.

She has presence, a voice from the cubicle said.

The three of them had gone to a restaurant to celebrate. Irene had come home announcing that the test tubes on her laboratory bench were displaying consistent silver rings, meaning life for certain sufferers. Erich had thrown aside his newspaper and leaped from his chair. "This calls for champagne!" he shouted, running out to buy her a rose. "You look beautiful," he enthused as he hailed a taxi.

Presence, the urinating woman said again, and then added: *For a Jew*.

Thea had flushed the toilet, then flushed it again to drown out anything more. "That one," she said loudly when she returned to the table.

Her father's face had a stricken bewildered look as if he had suddenly lost his way.

"Don't point, Thea," her mother said. "We are ordering dessert now, Erich. I am having the chocolate cake. Nothing is different from five minutes ago. People are human, no matter where they live. Did you really expect a miracle?"

He had. He had given up his beloved music. (He had a doctorate in Theory.) He had denied himself Goethe's words. In their place he looked at paintings because Germans were not noted for this art. He spoke only English, even at home. He never bought German products. With these sacrifices he thought he could avoid any recurrence. *You are a good man*, his wife had reminded him as their ship docked at the pier, but goodness was proving insufficient.

Later, remembering that dinner, Thea recalled a story from Irma, Irma who had become Thea's chronicler, her archivist. About a wet afternoon in Rome when a gypsy grabbed Erich's wrist and his goodness deserted him as well. The gypsy had dug her fingers into his skin. He was holding an umbrella slanted against the rain so he missed her approach. She had taken him by surprise. She wanted money, of course. She was small and thin, no more than a girl, but she carried a scrawny baby in a sling, the way one cradles a broken arm. He had jerked his hand trying to free himself but the gypsy hung on, looking up at him with a loathing he knew existed but not the inner freedom to so freely express it. When she let go he walked rapidly down the wide street and at the first fountain took off his suit coat, rolled up his sleeves and plunged his arms in the cold water clear to the elbow. Even after washing his wrist over and over, he still felt the pressure of her fingers.

"I thought you might have felt some sympathy," Irene said when he returned to their hotel room. But he had not. He felt only hatred and disgust. He refused supper and went immediately to bed.

"You didn't see her face," he told his wife at breakfast and never spoke of it again.

After their death Irma moved permanently into the Winters' apartment. Erich and Irene's will named Irma as guardian and provided amply for her to do it well. The arrangement was perfect under the circumstances. Thea loved Irma and Irma Thea. Irma kept Thea on the continuum of holiday dinners and collective vacations in the country. Under Irma's care Thea proceeded normally with life. She went to high school, Saturday afternoon movies, sweet-sixteen parties. She attended university. She wrote for the school newspaper, marched for civil rights, obtained her B.A., did a Master's. She fell in love several times, and then married. They moved to Canada (it was 1968 and he was draftable). In Canada Thea easily switched to -our endings, voted by ridings, reversed her patriotism in the War of 1812. She tried hard to understand all the implications of the War Measures Act. She did these things with the rationalism she inherited from her mother. With her father's extravagance she had six children.

There was a precedent for this lapse. When her parents died, Thea created a small second world and lived this secretive double life for many months. She had been angry with her parents for deserting her by dying and guilty over this anger. To cover up, she invented a tale. In it Irene was pregnant, erasing the largest vacancy in Thea's childhood. If the Danish trainman at the switches had not been drunk Thea would have had the brother she felt she deserved, possibly one of many. She made up a post-card from Erich.

Dear THEA: It is amazing what one hears from up here. The view, too, is splendid. Your mother is fine. She sends her regards and wishes you to know she is very pleased with the A you received in social studies. She also wants you to know that she is sorry that now you will not have a brother. She almost managed to give you one but he is up here with us, although he does not look very much like you or anyone else for that matter. Nothing grows up here, you see, and he still had a ways to go to be a real baby. He observes you, however, sees what you are doing, laughs with you, and feels sorry that you fell down. He hopes your arm will soon be better but thinks the cast makes you look important.

She kept a picture of a foetus, sinfully ripped from a public library book, in the bottom drawer of her desk. Every night before going to sleep she looked at the picture, at the veined skin, the giant twisted snake of a cord emanating from his belly, the hairy brow, the single opened eye focused on her (though she preferred to avoid this eye, it was so creepy), the forefinger of his right hand thoughtfully touching his lips. He seemed to be contemplating her, seeing through to her guilty heart. Perhaps he mulled over some gruesome act, some form of punishment, for this was not a picture of a kindly child. After a few months Thea grew afraid of him. She tore the picture into pieces and threw them down the incinerator shaft. Then she went back to the apartment and removed the photograph she kept on her night table. It showed a windy day at a lake somewhere, Irene's hair swept back, her dress billowing so that you could, if you wanted to, believe her stomach swelled slightly above her slim and shapely legs. Thea returned this photograph to its empty square of pasted corners and undid another: Erich and Irene, arm in arm in front of the Louvre, no breeze, just her parents as they were, with their noble posture and fine clothes, looking at the camera with that touch of hauteur, at ease, comfortable in their surroundings, displaying none of that baffled countenance that plagues tourists like a skin disease, Erich hatless for once, an inch shorter than his flat-bellied wife.

Nothing in this photograph indicated the risks her parents took, their arrogance, the noses they thumbed at a God no one in this story believed in any longer. It was about this time, flushing the pieces of the photograph down the incinerator shaft, that Thea lost any idea of an inhabited afterlife, a spot on the celestial map capable of communication, of soothing. She replaced this site with the starless sky of a cloudy night at the converted farm, the farmhouse lights blazing making the sky even blacker, creating a void. She felt vindicated to stumble upon this truth, but lost. Years later, looking at this photograph of her parents outside the Louvre, Thea still could bring up all the old anger. They should not be smiling so contentedly. They should rather be thinking of *her* needs, of the results to *her* of all this parading about a decrepit continent, a territory overripe like bad fruit, pestilences bursting through its skin: wars, plagues, inquisitions, concentration camps, train wrecks, any carnage will do. Erich's genes asserting themselves, survivors' genes, embedded with loneliness and the panicky inability to trust.

In 1990 Thea was forty-five. That summer she and her husband took the three younger children on what they had come to call *hors d'oeuvring*: whetting the appetite, a modern grand tour timed to fit into a restrictive late-twentieth-century summer holiday. Spotting, her husband said. Spot this. Spot that. Raising guffaws from Thea and the two girls. We Will Never Make Much of a Stain (travelling in such a whirlwind) became the trip's motto.

The adult Thea, Irene's daughter, explained away her adolescent ravings about the continent as a product of grief. She could acknowledge now without rancour the educational worth of ancient buildings, crumbling histories as food for the mind. *One cannot by rights blame a fractured column for human failings*, she proposed. *Occasionally one can make a case for nostalgia.* Yet Thea's itinerary isolated Germany as thoroughly as had Erich's. *Germany is an acquired taste and I have not acquired it*, she stubbornly insisted.

But one night, the sloping two-star hotel bed throwing them together, Thea confessed to her husband that she felt some sense of homecoming to be in Europe, albeit a disorienting homecoming, as if in her absence her town had been emptied and then repopulated with strangers, unrecognizable, but with familiar habits. She found herself gazing soberly at faces, at noses, moustaches, at those with darker skin, although she did not know what she looked for. She had ample opportunity for widespread examination. The methodology for these trips with their children (this one was a repeat of that taken with the three oldest several years before) called for nibbles, a bite of Paris and post-Franco Barcelona, a few crumbs of Nice and Monte Carlo, a slightly more generous serving of Florence, Rome, and Venice, before heading into the Swiss Alps, over to Amsterdam, across the Channel. On their second day in London Thea's husband suggested taking the children to the Tower. Thea begged off, saying she was up to here with history advanced by torture and the waylaying of travellers, and needed a break.

She took the Tube with them, but got out at Blackfriars. She would walk along the Embankment. The sky was overcast but showed no inclination to punish further. She had left her umbrella at the hotel. She felt this a day to be without encumbrances, although, since it was foolish to be completely unprepared, she carried her plastic travel raincoat folded to a minimum tucked inside her purse.

At forty-five Thea was a year younger than her parents were when they died. She would soon, barring the unforeseen, surpass them, experience life at ages they never enjoyed. Her parents appeared through the haze of childhood recollections and from remembrances by Irma and the others filtered as well by time and perception, and perhaps by what is most important, sentimentality at the early death. Thea's friends, people of her own age, had much clearer images of their parents, full of short-term memories, though some might argue this vision was equally skewed, favouring age this time, a time of complaints, the complaints coming full circle, echoing those of childhood.

Was this any better?

Thea leaned on the railing and regarded the Thames much like her parents stood on the deck of the *Siluria* and regarded the East River. In 1940 Erich and Irene were not yet orphans, were still to become survivors. But surely as they gazed at the dark, oily water melting the snow, they must have sensed the finiteness of the memories they carried, sealing them with this voyage, how there would be no additions. Seventeen years later they flung their daughter out the window into the wind, preserving the dilemma.

Thea left the river and plunged vaguely northwest, towards Trafalgar Square. She found the buildings in this part of London gloomy, defeated, as if the architects suffered from depression. If nothing caught her eye she could spend the afternoon at the National. She walked aimlessly. At each intersection she chose the street that most appealed to her. In a pub called the Queen's Mug, she drank a surprisingly good cappuccino. She bought a pasty from a street vendor and munched it as she walked. In a small sidestreet, more accurately an alley, she came upon a sandwich board announcing a lunchtime concert. The board directed her down a passageway between two shops that led to a small park surrounded by a high wrought-iron fence. In the centre was a church with a disproportionately tall steeple and a set of smudged columns tarting up the entrance. A few bushes and one tree valiantly attempted to keep up appearances. The concert, the sandwich board declared, was a memorial, honouring one Richard Basefield Morris, OBE. The public was welcome. The music was Mahler.

They were to play the *Funf Lieder nach Rukert*, the Second Symphony's final movement, and a tone poem Mahler wrote for his wife, Alma. The tone poem, the program stated, had been discovered only in 1947, stuck between pages 25 and 26 of a German translation of Shakespeare's *Julius Caesar*, purchased in a used-book store by a man in Leeds.

Had Erich Winter known of this discovery? Had the great conductor, Bruno Walter, who was often in New York, telephoned with the news hoping with the war over to rekindle Erich's spirit? Who could she ask? Irma was dead. The others might remember, but their numbers too had dwindled and because she lived so far away they exchanged only ritual messages, Happy Birthday, Happy New Year, she wrote, always Happy, although their existence with its cancers and its incontinence must be far from that. Would they remember a detail about her father and The Marrano, as Erich had labelled Mahler for their amusement because the composer had converted to Catholicism to become acceptable. Thea found a seat in a side row of pews.

The church interior was as dingy as the outside columns had been. Tattered banners hung above the aisle looking in age and condition like leftovers from a medieval joust. As if to offset this tawdriness, the concert's program was modern and well-designed, encased in a stiff paper folder, the graphics transposed, one cover positive, one negative. On the front Mahler bore the wild look of a man terrified of the abyss. On the back the same man gazed benignly, though sternly, demanding one remember they were here to celebrate life and death and to meditate upon what lies beyond. Thea sat quietly, stiffly, with the same single-minded desire of herself as a child in bed, convinced a thief stalked the apartment, to not disturb. She did not like churches. They made her feel more ill-placed than normal. Out of this discomfort she let her eyes examine her

surroundings hoping for relief. She passed on a renaissance por-
trait of Mary and Joseph, hand in hand – Being married? Mary
looked decidedly pregnant – and looking upward towards the
ceiling was rewarded by a fat naked angel reclining amongst the
organ pipes. Someone with a sense of humour had painted this
angel. He was a lurid gold, and he appraised the congregation
below him with a mortal and decidedly contemptuous smile.
Silently Thea saluted the angel and felt his acknowledgement.
He would be a grand conversationalist, she felt. She wished him
animate and was suddenly at ease.

A young man wearing a crew-neck sweater over a shirt and tie
came out from a small door by the altar and welcomed them.

"Forgive us for being only ten musicians," he began apologetically, "but we are a spirited ten. And there is a full choir,
thanks to St. Stephen's, so you need not feel cheated. We chose
this particular program because Richard loved Mahler and had
been instrumental in persuading the *Concise Oxford Dictionary
of Music* to write a less disdainful conclusion about Britain's
appreciation of this marvellous composer. After the concert we
invite all his friends to take refreshments with us in the hall."

The anecdotes that followed were affectionate. It was that
type of occasion. Thea's favourite was Richard Basefield Morris's
demand for punctuality so that once he began a choral society
meeting with only himself in attendance. As the musicians
assembled and tuned she wondered about anecdotes of Erich
Winter, if this were his memorial. Bemused comments on the
bird's nest hair and pitch black coffee, on his trademark hat and
decent record as husband and father. A retelling as allegory of
the Roman gypsy's bruise on his wrist. A paragraph about his
disconnectedness, followed by a summary of his love and hate
for Mahler, who under the circumstances he had been unable to
forgive, rejecting his music and all music, which had been his
greatest pleasure, as a punishment to himself.

"I am lost to the world," the contralto sang from the first
Lieder.

Erich Winter poring over snapshots with a magnifying glass,
desperate to find a face, a single face, that he recognized, a
face that had denied chance. That had cheated on that family

gathering. Erich's mother cutting up the stationery from his father's haberdashery, unusable since the shop had been confiscated by the Nazis, cutting twenty-three slips, one for each of Erich and Irene's generation. *Our decision*, the older members of the family stated firmly. *Not to be argued with*. The prize of this lottery was emigration, provided by an uncle who years before had settled in America. The elders had decided that if the person who selected the slip marked X was married the spouse would automatically go as well. If the winner was unmarried, the lottery would be repeated with nine slips of paper, one of each of the remaining unmarried cousins. The Americans demanded cash up front for their affidavits. The uncle could afford to sponsor only two. *Forgive me*, he had written.

Erich's mother passed around the cut-glass bowl. The cousins kept the papers folded until everyone had chosen. They opened them at the same time.

If the uncle had been a wealthy man Thea would have been part of a large and boisterous congregation (although a lopsided one because Irene had been an only child, as if her family lacked the instinct for species survival). Erich's relations fill the marbled photo albums he kept in the cupboard in his bedroom. Their energy, their vigour spilled from the old felt pages. They climbed mountains in packs. They romped on the lawn in bathing suits. They turned hoses on one another. In winter they strolled along the frozen river in coats with fur collars. Or they went skiing. On holidays at the beach they arranged themselves in a group, forcing the photographer to stand so far away it was sometimes difficult to make out the faces.

On one page in one of these forbidden albums her parents leap-frogged over a line of Erich's cousins.

This is the most accurate picture, Erich once said. *Irene and I making an early exit, pushing the others back, climbing over them in our haste to get away.*

The storm of the Second Symphony broke over the church. A torrent of drums and horns, increasing to a gale. The end of the world. Final retribution. A logical passage from a composer who lost his daughter, his job, his health, his religion, and at an unfairly young age, his life. *I sympathize*, Thea said silently, directing her comment to the angel whom she imagined as a messenger. The angel did not alter his expression but his gold finger seemed to move, just slightly, but enough to make her look at the makeshift stage.

And yes, if you squinted in the already dim light of this soiled church you could imagine that the seated musicians and the singers standing behind them are a family gathering grouped for the inevitable photograph. While the music swelled round her, while the choir sang: "I shall die to live" – too melodramatic for Thea, but fitting for the moment – she assigned names to the faces, her grandmother to the cellist, her grandfather to the bearded singer fourth from the left, until she invoked all the aunts, uncles, cousins, whose names she discovered she had memorized.

"Believe, my heart, you have lost nothing," the same contralto of the *Lieder* sang.

Only a desperate man would write music to such nonsense. Thea did not feel desperate but she would take up the offer of the young man in the sweater for refreshments in the hall after the concert. She had never met Richard Basefield Morris but neither did she ever know the Winters or the uncle already in America or any of the countless cousins. In the hall she will smile, make small talk, pretend for a moment she is at a family reunion. Why she should have been visited by an angel of all things, in a church of all places, she promised not to ask. Such things happen. She was not one to waste opportunities. She was here to rest her father's spirit, to leave it off its wanderings. The golden angel would help, would light just for a moment that black void. Erich she knew would have loved this angel, the gaudy penis, the idle pose, the ironical smile. The three of them would drink coffee, no milk, no sugar, their chairs arranged on the same side of the table so that they could enjoy the piazza and then they would go their separate ways. *Dear THEA, Your mother has finally given birth* . . .

In the pause between resurrection and Mahler's love song for Alma, Thea heard again the roar of London traffic.

About the Authors

Michelle Alfano is a Toronto writer and literary editor of a cultural magazine. Her short stories and non-fiction pieces have been featured in numerous literary journals and cultural magazines. She is currently completing a collection of short stories featuring some of the characters who appear in "Opera."

Mary Borsky is from the Peace River country in northern Alberta. She has published stories in various magazines, and anthologies including *The Macmillan Anthology* and *Best Canadian Stories*. "Maps of the Known World" is one story from *Influence of the Moon*, which will be published by Porcupine's Quill in fall 1995. She lives in Ottawa.

Gabriella Goliger is originally from Montreal, but has lived in Jerusalem, Iqaluit, NWT, and currently resides in Ottawa. Her work has appeared in the anthology *Tide Lines: Stories of Change by Lesbians* (Gynergy Books, 1991) and in *Our Lives: Lesbian Personal Writings* (Second Story Press, 1991). She is currently working on a collection of stories based on the lives of ordinary people who survived extraordinary times.

Elizabeth Hay has written *Crossing the Snow Line* (1989), *The Only Snow in Havana* (1992), and *Captivity Tales: Canadians in New York* (1993). "Hand Games" is part of a new manuscript called *The Small Change of Friendship*. She lives in Ottawa.

Shaena Lambert grew up in Vancouver and is now living in Toronto where she works as a freelance writer. She has published stories in *Prism international* and *The North American Review*, and commentary on peace and environmental issues in *The Globe and Mail*, *Toronto Star*, Montreal *Gazette*, and *Ottawa Citizen*. She is currently writing a book of short stories.

Elise Levine is co-winner of the 1994 *Prism international* Short Fiction Contest. Her work has appeared in various publications, including *The Malahat Review*, *Quarry*, *Canadian Fiction Magazine*, and *Coming Attractions '94*. Her short-story collection, Driving Men Mad, has recently been published by the Porcupine's Quill. Elise Levine lives in Toronto, where she is currently at work on a novel.

Roger Burford Mason is a Toronto writer, editor, and broadcaster. He has published two collections of short stories (Hounslow Press, 1990 and 1992), and has written a biography of Franz Johnston, the elusive founder-member of the Group of Seven, which will be published by Quarry Press in 1995. A third collection of short stories, *Radio Days*, will be published by Hounslow Press in 1996, and a book about the arcane history and practices of fishing, illustrated by wood-engraver Wesley Bates, will be published by the Porcupine's Quill in time for the opening of the trout season in 1996.

Antanas Sileika's first novel, *Dinner at the End of the World* was published by Mosaic Press in 1994. "Going Native" is the first chapter of his nearly completed new novel, *Buying on Time*. In addition to fiction, his non-fiction has been published in publications as diverse as *The Globe and Mail* and *Saturday Night*. He has written radio comedy and drama and is a freelance broadcaster.

Kathryn Woodward was born and raised in New York, lived for some years in Africa and Micronesia and then emigrated with her family to British Columbia. She currently works as an X-ray technician. Her stories have been published in *Descant*, *Event*, *Carolina Quarterly*, and *The Malahat Review*. In 1992, she won *Fiddlehead*'s Better Homes and Gardens contest.

About the Contributing Journals

The Antigonish Review, now entering its twenty-second year of publication, features poetry, fiction, reviews, and critical articles from all parts of Canada, the U.S., and overseas. It promotes new and established authors. Each issue contains the work of twenty to thirty poets, five or six fiction writers, reviews of ten to fifteen books, and two or three articles directed at a general audience. Original graphics are used extensively to enliven the format. Editor: George Sanderson. Submissions and correspondence: St. Francis Xavier University, Antigonish, Nova Scotia, B2G 1C0.

The Capilano Review has been published out of Capilano College's Humanities Division since 1972. It is a tri-annual magazine of the arts, publishing poetry, fiction, fine art, and drama from all over Canada and the world. It has been recognized for excellence five times by the National Magazine Awards and been cited by the Canadian Studies Association. Its distribution spans nine countries. Subscriptions are $25 for one year (three issues). Write to: *The Capilano Review* c/o Capilano College, 2055 Purcell Way, North Vancouver, B.C., V7J 3H5. Telephone: (604) 984-1712, Fax: (604) 983-7520.

Descant is a quarterly literary magazine which publishes poetry, prose, fiction, interviews, travel pieces, letters, photographs, engravings, art, and literary criticism. Editor: Karen Mulhallen. Managing Editor: Tracy Jenkins. Submissions and correspondence: P.O. Box 314, Station P, Toronto, Ontario, M5S 2S8.

Exile is a quarterly magazine which features Canadian fiction and poetry as well as the work of writers in translation from all over the world; some the best-known, others unknown. Publisher and Editor: Barry Callaghan. Submissions and correspondence: Box 67, Station B, Toronto, Ontario, M5T 2C0.

Fireweed is a feminist quarterly committed to an editorial policy of cultural diversity. Existing for twelve years as a collective organization of women, *Fireweed* is determined to publish literary and cultural works from a feminist grass roots perspective. It accepts unsolicited submissions from all women and does not publish material considered racist, sexist, or homophobic. Guest collectives have produced some of *Fireweed*'s best issues, such as "Class Is the Issue," "Lesbiantics," and "Asian Women." *Fireweed* welcomes ideas for future theme issues. For subscription information, or to send in submissions, write to *Fireweed*, P.O. Box 279, Station B, Toronto, Ontario, M5T 2W2, or call (416) 323-9512.

The Malahat Review publishes mostly fiction and poetry and includes a substantial review article in each issue. We are open to dramatic works, so long as they lend themselves to the page; we welcome literary works that defy easy generic categorization. Editor: Derk Wynand. Associate Editor: Marlene Cookshaw. Assistant Editor: Lucy Bashford. Submissions and correspondence: University of Victoria, P.O. Box 1700, MS 8524, Victoria, B.C., V8W 2Y2.

For more than thirty years, *Prism international* has published work by writers both new and established, Canadian and international. Edited by graduate students of creative writing at the University of British Columbia, *Prism* looks for innovative fiction, poetry, drama, as well as creative non-fiction, in English or English translation. The 1995/6 editorial board will consist of Leah Postman as Editor; Andrew Gray as Executive Editor; Annabel Lyon as Fiction Editor, and Jennifer Herbison as Poetry Editor. *Prism* also holds an annual fiction contest. Request guidelines or send submissions to: The Editors, *Prism international*, Department of Creative Writing, BUCH E462 – 1866 Main Mall, University of British Columbia, Vancouver, B.C., V6T 1Z1. E-mail: prism@unixg.ubc.ca.

Quarry magazine, founded in 1952, continues to publish short fiction, poetry, essays, and reviews of any length or style by writers new or established from anywhere in Canada and abroad. Publisher: Bob Hilderley. Editor: Mary Cameron, with a board of associate editors. Submissions and correspondence: P.O. Box 1061, Kingston, Ontario, K7L 4Y5.

Submissions were received from the following journals:

The Antigonish Review
(Antigonish, N.S.)

Grain
(Regina, Sask.)

Blood & Aphorisms
(Toronto, Ont.)

Green's Magazine
(Regina, Sask.)

Canadian Fiction Magazine
(Kingston, Ont.)

Kairos
(Hamilton, Ont.)

The Capilano Review
(North Vancouver, B.C.)

The Malahat Review
(Victoria, B.C.)

Dalhousie Review
(Halifax, N.S.)

Matrix
(Montreal, Que.)

Descant
(Toronto, Ont.)

NeWest
(Saskatoon, Sask.)

Event
(New Westminster, B.C.)

The New Quarterly
(Waterloo, Ont.)

Exile
(Toronto, Ont.)

Other Voices
(Edmonton, Alta.)

The Fiddlehead
(Fredericton, N.B.)

Parchment
(London, Ont.)

Fireweed
(Toronto, Ont.)

Prairie Fire
(Winnipeg, Man.)

Prairie Journal Trust
(Calgary, Alta.)

Prism international
(Vancouver, B.C.)

Quarry
(Kingston, Ont.)

Queen's Quarterly
(Kingston, Ont.)

TickleAce
(St. John's, Nfld.)

The Windsor Review
(Windsor, Ont.)

WRIT
(Toronto, Ont.)

The Journey Prize Anthology
List of Previous Contributing Authors

* Winners of the $10,000 Journey Prize

5

1993

Caroline Adderson, "Oil and Dread"
David Bergen, "La Rue Prevette"
Marina Endicott, "With the Band"
Dayv James-French, "Cervine"
Michael Kenyon, "Durable Tumblers"
K. D. Miller, "A Litany in Time of Plague"
Robert Mullen, "Flotsam"
Gayla Reid, "Sister Doyle's Men"*
Oakland Ross, "Bang-bang"
Robert Sherrin, "Technical Battle for Trial Machine"
Carol Windley, "The Etruscans"

6

1994

Anne Carson, "Water Margins: An Essay on Swimming by
    My Brother"
Richard Cumyn, "The Sound He Made"
Genni Gunn, "Versions"
Melissa Hardy, "Long Man the River"*
Robert Mullen, "Anomie"
Vivian Payne, "Free Falls"
Jim Reil, "Dry"
Robyn Sarah, "Accept My Story"
Joan Skogan, "Landfall"
Dorothy Speak, "Relatives in Florida"
Alison Wearing, "Notes from Under Water"